The Love Rock Chronicle

By Pat Kaufman and Tony See

DEDICATION

Pat Kaufman: To Kathy and Clint, Beth and Mike, and especially Lou

Tony See: Thank you to my beautiful wife Denise and my son Anthony for your love and inspiration. I dedicate this book to Roger Herring. Thank you for all the love lessons you taught me over the years. You will never be forgotten and your Love will always live on....Love Rocks!

ABOUT THE AUTHORS

Pat Kaufman is an attorney and freelance writer. She is the author of a previous children's book, *Something Small For Christmas.* She lives in Southern Maryland with her family.

Tony See is a commercial general contractor with a passion and great love for the outdoors. His Love Rock collecting has enriched his and many other's lives. He believes everyone can use more appreciation and love around them. He has had very powerful experiences sharing Love Rocks with others and wants it to continue beyond his own path.

ACKNOWLEDGEMENT

Book Cover by Sarah Rosenthal

CHAPTER 1

Henry could not remember a worse day, ever, at school.

Granted, he was the new kid so he didn't have any friends, but still, this day was one for the books. He turned the corner, and scuffed along the last block leading to the small cul de sac where his modest rental house was located. Even now, two months since he and his mom had moved there after his father died, he still didn't think of it as home. He shivered in the brisk air as the sunlight faded in the early September afternoon. How he missed his old house, his old friends, his old school – but most of all, how he missed his dad.

Henry reviewed the day's events, giving them a mental sort-through from bad to worst. The worst surely had to be the discovery of the dead, rotting fish in his locker. He had no idea that a fish smell could permeate everything in a locker so quickly. Even his history book still smelled like fish, and it had been on the top shelf!

Then there was the daily conversation with Colby Crane, the burly captain of the school football team. Colby dedicated a portion of each day to gathering a group of players to watch his taunting chats with Henry. When it first started, Henry actually thought Colby was trying to be friendly, but he soon learned better. Today, wearing his ubiquitous practice jersey, with the big captain's "C" sewn on the front, Colby had found Henry standing in front of his locker, surveying the smelly mess.

"Anyone ever tell you that you smell like a fish, Caldwell?" Colby asked, not a bit surprised about the presence of the fish. Henry knew instantly that some of the football players were behind this prank.

Henry was well aware that there was nothing to be gained in answering questions from a bully. But he was exasperated and the rotten fish had taken him off guard. "It's not me that smells, it's my locker!" he exclaimed.

This was apparently the most hilarious thing that the collective football gang had ever heard, and they exploded in mocking laughter. Henry noticed a few high fives among the team members, which made him all the more sure that they had put the fish into his locker.

Colby was not finished. He and Henry were about the same height, but Colby outweighed Henry by at least 30 pounds. Colby eyed Henry's wiry frame with a slight sneer, giving Henry's shoulder a supposedly playful, but actually painful, punch. "Walk on tryouts for the football team start tomorrow, Caldwell," he announced. "Are you in?"

Henry sighed and this time kept it simple. "No." He pushed his glasses, which had been dislodged by the punch, back up onto his nose.

"I bet you never played a sport in your life, Henry" Colby said derisively. "I bet you throw a football like a girl. That is, if you've ever even held a football. You do know what a football is, don't you? It's this brown pigskin-covered object that real men use." He rolled his eyes at his teammates, who nodded appreciatively at this brilliant commentary.

Henry, despite his better instincts, rose to the bait. "I do play a sport, as a matter of fact," he answered indignantly. "I fence."

"You fence?" Colby asked, feigning surprise. "You mean you sell stolen goods?" He and his band of behemoths laughed uproariously. Of course they understood exactly what Henry meant, and knew that he was not really an illegal "fence" that buys stolen property to sell it later, but this answer was too good not to make fun of. A few of the guys pretended to fence with each other, yelling "on guard," and standing on their tippy toes to make it seem the most prissy of sports.

Finally, they tired of making fun of Henry. "C'mon guys, we've got to go practice a real sport," Colby commanded.

"So long, Zorro," he said, flinging this final insult over his shoulder as the guys lumbered off, "maybe an athlete of your caliber should try out for the glee club."

Relieved that the daily ordeal was over, Henry turned back to his odoriferous locker. He was so engrossed in trying not to gag from the smell as he tried to figure out what to do with the fish that he didn't even realize that someone was standing next to him. He actually jumped when the girl spoke.

"They really are a bunch of dimwits," she said, shaking her head as the last of team disappeared from sight. She extended her hand, thoughtful enough to make no comment about the stench of fish and added, "My name is Emily Stone. Do you really fence?"

"W-w-well, yes, I mean, I do, that is, uhhh, nice to meet you," Henry said in a rush, realizing to his dismay that he sounded like a world-class dimwit himself. He shook her hand, feeling distinctly less than suave as he nervously adjusted his glasses. But in his confusion, and even surrounded by the smell of fish, he knew that this was the nicest thing that had happened to him since he had come to this new school.

CHAPTER 2

Henry unlocked the door and walked into his empty house. It was small and cramped, a far cry from the comfortable home that he had shared with his mom and dad until the car accident changed everything.

But there was no time to think about that now. His mom would not get home from work until nearly 7:00, and she had left food on the kitchen counter for him to prepare for the oven. She had also left a little snack for him. He grabbed the bag of chocolate covered pretzels and dried apricots and sat at the kitchen table, enjoying the unexpected treat. With money as scarce as it was, even snacks had become a luxury in his suddenly diminished life.

He reviewed his mom's instructions one last time. "Preheat oven to 350, add carrots and beans and put the casserole in the oven at 6 so it will be ready when I come home. I love you. Mom." He read those last four words over one more time as he finished the last pretzel. I love you. Mom. That was the only thing that kept him going.

Once the casserole was ready, Henry went up to his room. He knew he should start his homework, but he just didn't feel like it. Instead, he slipped on his fencing mask and picked up his épée, taking pleasure in the heft of the triangular blade, perfectly balanced in his hand. For a few blissful minutes he imagined himself in a bout, standing on the piste, or fencing strip, saluting both his opponent and the referee in the time-honored tradition of fencing. And then, as the referee called, "en garde," he advanced in a rush, scoring an immediate touch. Henry had to laugh at how easy it was to win imaginary bouts. He turned the blade over in his hand and laid it down. This was just a daydream. Fencing, he realized, was just one more thing he had lost.

The quiet house felt empty and lonely, just like Henry himself. He opened his math book and got to work, keeping an eye on the clock so as not to forget that casserole. But his thoughts kept straying to Emily, the first and to be honest, only person who had been nice to him at school. Don't get your hopes up he thought to himself, she's probably already forgotten about you. He recalled his dumb stammering comments to her and made a mental note to try not to sound like a complete dope next time. Assuming there was a next time, which there probably wouldn't be because why would Emily Stone, whom he personally found quite pretty come to think about it, even give him the time of day. No point in setting himself up for another disappointment. Starting tomorrow, he vowed to himself, he would be cool and aloof and act like he didn't need a friend in the world. Because, as he told himself firmly, he didn't.

Emily, who also lived within walking distance of school, had been thinking about Henry as she strolled back to her own home. She had been disgusted as she watched Colby and his gang make fun of Henry, and she wondered if she should have tried to stop it. But confronting half the football team was…she mulled it over…was what? She couldn't decide but an insistent voice inside told her that just standing and watching had not been her finest moment. One thing she did know, though – there was something about Henry Caldwell that she liked. She vowed to herself that she would make a real effort to get to know him better.

CHAPTER 3

As fate would have it, neither Henry nor Emily got the chance to use their opposing plans of action for a couple of weeks. Besides the fact that they were in different classes, Emily was busy after school with the school newspaper, as the time for publication of the quarterly edition was nearing.

Henry, on the other hand, had no after school activities to go to. He would have loved to write for the school paper, but when the list was going around he felt too shy to put his own name down. For days afterward he was disappointed with himself, but now he was just as glad. Colby's bullying was steadily sapping what little self-esteem he had left, and he had just about convinced himself that he would have been a complete failure as a reporter.

The only good thing was that, with football tryouts and practices going strong, Colby and his teammates were too busy to pay any attention to Henry. The irony of all this was not lost on Henry. Here he had decided to be cool and aloof and no one was the least bit interested in whether he was cool and aloof or not. Or even, he thought morosely, whether he existed at all.

The sound of the last bell on Friday afternoons always came as a great relief. Henry relished the thought of two whole days with no one around to remind him that he was as alone as he had ever been in his life.

He gathered his books and stuffed them into his backpack as quickly as he could, ignored by the throngs of students milling about, discussing their plans for getting together over the weekend. He could hear what they were saying, as they made jokes and ribbed each other the way only good friends can do, and he actually had to will himself not to cry. Not that anyone would have noticed, but regardless, he made a supreme effort to choke back his tears. At least he still had a little pride left.

CHAPTER 4

It was such a beautiful fall day when he arrived home from school Henry knew he didn't want to spend it indoors. He decided to take a walk and explore his new neighborhood. Energized by the crisp fall air, he sprinted to his back porch and shed his backpack, not even bothering to go into the house. He was just starting to walk away when he heard a whimpering sound. He stopped in his tracks. What could that be?

Henry circled back into his yard, trying to trace the sound. Nothing.

He had just about convinced himself that he was imagining things when he heard the sound again. There was no imagining this! Someone or something was in trouble.

Henry positioned himself in the middle of the yard and stood quietly, listening as intently as he ever had. Nothing....nothing........ nothing. Nothing but silence.

Henry's patience had run out. He started off on his walk and was nearly out of the yard when he heard it again. A low moan just off to his left. Henry moved slowly in the direction of the sound, his heart beating wildly. Something was going on.

And then he saw it. A ball of wriggling fur trapped in a shallow underground drain. Henry instinctively reached down and retrieved the animal, not sure what it might be.

It was a dog, a little beagle, shivering and whimpering. Henry cradled it in his lap, wondering how this dog had come to be here in this place, so alone. Welcome to the club, he thought.

The dog had so completely relaxed in Henry's warm embrace that it had actually fallen asleep. "You are one lucky dog," he said softly, as he scratched the soft fur between two very big floppy ears. Henry shuddered to think what would have happened if he hadn't found the dog that afternoon. "Yep, one very lucky dog," he repeated, not realizing that he had just named his new friend. Or that the little beagle wasn't the only lucky one that fine fall day.

Henry sat on the top step of the back porch and stroked the brown and black flecked fur, trying to figure out how he could convince his mom to let him keep this little guy. He knew it would be an uphill battle for the one reason that had dictated most everything in their lives since his dad died – not enough money.

11

The dog awoke and immediately started gnawing gently on Henry's hand, clearly starving. Henry tried to think what to do. He didn't want to bring the dog into the house quite yet; it didn't seem fair to his mom to be sneaky. And what should he do with the dog while he went into the house to get some food? Tie it up? But with what?

Henry decided on a simple plan. He would leave the dog on the back porch while he fetched a bowl of half milk, half water and some leftover chicken that he had had his eye on for himself. If the dog ran away while he was inside, so be it – some things you wish for are not meant to be, as he was only too well aware. But it didn't keep him from offering some encouragement as he closed the kitchen door, "Don't go away, Lucky, I'll be right back with dinner."

Henry needn't have worried. The dog not only didn't leave, but he scratched insistently at the door until Henry returned with his supper. The chicken disappeared quickly and the milk mixture was clearly a good choice, as there was not a drop left in the bowl when the dog finally looked up, licking his lips as he ambled over, ready to be held.

While Henry had been in the kitchen, he had noticed the message light blinking on the phone. He pushed the button. It was his mom. "Henry, honey, I'm going to be late tonight. I got some overtime! The extra money will really help. I think I see a dinner out in our future this weekend!"

Just a few minutes ago this message would have plunged Henry into a deep sadness and he would have spent the evening alone feeling sorry for himself. But now it really didn't bother him at all. He knew he had a friend, waiting right outside the kitchen door.

Actually, Henry was glad to have the extra time so that he could devise a plan for keeping the dog safe and warm – and hidden, of course – until he could, somehow, get his mom to agree to let Lucky stay. First, though, Henry got some boards and covered the drainage hole so there would be no more accidents. When he finished his work, he sat down on the kitchen stoop to think. Lucky came over and nestled close to him. Henry had not felt this good in months. They stayed outdoors until the sun disappeared and darkness fell.

CHAPTER 5

Mary Caldwell didn't pull into the driveway until nearly 10 p.m. and she had mixed emotions as she put the car in park and shut off the engine. On the one hand, getting overtime work was a godsend and, tired as she was, it had felt good to watch the extra hours, and the extra money, pile up. But on the other hand, she knew how tough her long absence was on Henry.

She sat quietly in the car for a few minutes, steeling herself against going in and finding Henry sad and upset, as he always was when she was late. She didn't blame him. A lot had changed for both of them in the blink of an eye and there were many days when she wondered how either of them had managed to move forward as well as they did. With a long sigh, she opened the car door and started up the walkway.

To her surprise, Henry wasn't in sight. He always waited up for her in the living room, usually with the TV on, though he was far more likely to be doing something on his dad's old laptop, his prized possession, than watching a television show. Could he have gone to bed? He never went to bed before she got home, no matter how late. She ran upstairs, but his room was dark and empty. Mary felt panic rising in her chest as she raced back down the stairs, calling Henry's name. No answer.

She stood in the kitchen trying to calm herself down and think rationally. She had just decided to call 911 when the kitchen door opened and Henry came strolling in.

"Oh, hi mom," he said, obviously surprised to see her but more cheerful than she would ever have imagined. "I didn't know you were getting home so early."

"Henry," his mother tried to keep her voice steady but the fear that had yet to subside made her sound shrill, "where on EARTH have you been? It's 10 o'clock at night!"

Gosh, was it 10 already? Henry chastised himself for going out one last time to see Lucky. He had set up a comfortable little bed in the old rundown tool shed in the back yard, and he had been pleased to see that Lucky had snuggled deep into the packing quilt that Henry had spread in one of the shallow cardboard boxes left over from the move and was making himself very much at home.

"Well, I was, I mean, it's such a nice night I thought I would just go on out and, and… uh, check on, that is, I mean, look at the stars," he finished feebly, but it was the best he could do on the spur of the moment. She had really caught him off guard.

15

"The stars?" His mom opened the door and looked up at the night sky. Although a sliver of the half moon could occasionally be seen through the drifting clouds, there wasn't a star in sight. She turned back and looked at Henry closely. He looked guilty and seemed unusually happy. This could only mean one thing.

Mary was exhausted but she knew this was a conversation that couldn't wait until morning.

"Henry," she said in a measured tone, forcing herself to be calm. "Sit down. I know what's going on."

Henry was crushed. Obviously she knew about the dog – why hadn't he just told her in the first place, he thought ruefully. Now it was too late. He would look like a sneak and she'd never let him keep Lucky. He hung his head. How had she found out?

"Henry," his mother said as she took a seat beside him and made him look her in the eye. "You're using drugs, aren't you?"

There are some things that are impossible to fake, and pure, absolute, unadulterated astonishment is one of them. Henry looked so totally surprised at her question she knew in an instant that, whatever her son might have been doing out in the yard at 10 o'clock at night, it didn't involve drugs.

"Drugs??" Henry asked, so completely baffled that he honestly didn't know what else to say. He was hiding a dog! And his mom thought he was using drugs? How had it come to this?

Henry pulled himself together and suddenly felt a wave of relief. She didn't know about Lucky, after all! "Mom," he said, "of course, I don't use drugs. I don't even know how. Where would I even get them?"

Mary's relief was as palpable as Henry's. She was as sure that he wasn't using drugs as he was that she didn't know about Lucky. But, Henry thought to himself, shouldn't I just be honest about hiding a dog in the yard, and confess right now?

Henry wrestled with his conscience, but he could see the dark circles under his mother's eyes and he knew how tired she was. And he did feel bad about having scared her to death with his absence from the house. So, although just a few minutes ago he regretted not telling her about Lucky, now he made a command decision – the confession could wait for another day.

After his mom went to bed Henry was tempted to make one more trip to the shed, but he knew it was out of the question. That was all his mom would need, to catch him sneaking around in the back yard at midnight. He had settled Lucky in but he had not closed the shed door, so Lucky could walk off any time he wanted. As much as Henry had wanted to lock him in, something told him what mattered was not whether Lucky had to stay, but whether he wanted to stay.

CHAPTER 6

Saturday morning dawned bright and cool, a magnificently crisp fall day. Usually Henry slept in on Saturdays, but this morning he was up and dressed before 7 a.m. He knew his mom, after such a long night at work, would sleep soundly for a couple more hours and he wanted to feed Lucky and take him for walk before she got up. Assuming, of course, Lucky was still there. Henry looked out the window at the shed.

The door was ajar, just as he had left it.

Henry had done some research on the Internet on what to feed dogs. He quickly learned that it should be good quality dog food, but that was out of the question at this point. He had also learned that milk wasn't such a great idea, so Henry settled on water and some leftover meatloaf for Lucky's breakfast. He felt a little guilty about this diet of leftovers, but consoled himself with the knowledge that left to his own devices Lucky would have to scrounge for an even less nutritious meal.

It was very quiet inside the shed as Henry approached and he felt his heart start to sink. It had not even been 24 hours since he had found Lucky and he was already almost ill at the thought of losing him. With his hands full with the food and water, Henry had to turn sideways and push the door open a little wider with his foot. He slipped inside.

It took a few seconds for his eyes to adjust to the dim light. But even before he had completely acclimated it was clear that the packing box was empty. Henry put the food down and scanned the four corners of the little shed. Empty. Empty. Empty. Empty.

The disappointment was overwhelming. And suddenly everything seemed too much – the loss of his dad, Colby's taunts, the dead fish, the searing loneliness of the last few months, and now this. Unbidden, a sob escaped from Henry's throat, echoing loudly in the tiny shed.

The abrupt sound brought an immediate response. The quilt in the packing box started moving and soon, peeking out from under the covers, obviously startled out of a deep sleep, was Lucky. The dog's reaction was instant and heartfelt. Lucky raced toward Henry with his tail wagging furiously, and jumped into Henry's outstretched arms.

It's amazing how fast human emotions can swing. Henry had gone from disconsolate to jubilant in a matter of seconds. As he watched Lucky finish off the meatloaf and slurp noisily from his water bowl, Henry had the grace to recall that he had put his mother through the same emotional roller coaster last night as he experienced this morning when he thought he had lost Lucky. No doubt about it, he couldn't keep sneaking around like this and making his mom worry and be suspicious. Today would have to be the day of reckoning for Lucky.

CHAPTER 7

Henry scooped Lucky up and trotted quickly around to the front of the house and down the street to the end of the block. Once out of sight of his house he set Lucky down so they could take a walk. It would have been nice to have a leash, especially since there were laws about letting your dog roam free, but Lucky didn't have a collar and Henry didn't have a leash, so that was just one more thing that would have to go by the boards, for now. As they strolled along, Lucky roamed ahead or lagged behind, but never for long. He seemed most content simply to walk beside Henry, occasionally brushing up against Henry's leg as if to reassure himself Henry was still right there.

When they returned home, Henry got ready to put the next step of his plan into action.

First, he peeked into his mom's room and was relieved to find that she was still sound asleep. Her soft, rhythmic snoring reassured him that she was in a deep sleep and he fervently hoped her snooze would last for at least the next half hour.

Next, Henry tiptoed into the hall bathroom he and his mother shared. He noted with satisfaction that her hair dryer was on the small vanity, the very thing recommended for drying a dog. After getting two of the darkest colored towels he could find, he began to fill the bathtub. He dipped his hand in as the water started to accumulate, hoping it truly was lukewarm, which as Henry had also learned on his Internet search was perfect for a dog's bath.

When everything was ready Henry ran back and opened the kitchen door. Lucky was right there, waiting patiently on the top step.

Henry sat down and brought the little beagle close. He leaned in and whispered into the dog's floppy ear. "Listen, Lucky, if there is one thing my mom hates, it's dirt. She just has a thing about it. So, in the interest of making a great first impression, I think it's time you had a bath. But we have to be quiet about this – no barking in the house, okay?" Lucky seemed completely on board with the plan, and so with that admonition taken care of, they were off.

The bathroom was warm and steamy. Henry started by dipping his hand in the water and running it over Lucky's back, just to get him used to things. Then, as Lucky's eyes closed and he seemed to relax, Henry gently set him in the tub and reached for the shampoo.

The barking, reverberating off the tile walls, was as loud as anything Henry had ever heard. How was it possible for such a small dog to make such a racket? Henry scrambled to rub a little shampoo onto Lucky's coat and tried to quickly rinse him down. The barks turned to howls. Henry gave up and snatched Lucky out of the water, hoping to wrap him in a towel and calm him down. But Lucky wriggled free and shook himself vigorously, spraying dirty water everywhere.

The sharp raps on the bathroom door came as no surprise.

"HENRY," his mom yelled, "WHAT IS GOING ON IN THERE?"

Henry fell back on the universal answer of childhood. "N-Nothing, Mom," he said.

"Open. This. Door. This. Minute," his mom ordered, through clenched teeth.

Lucky had quieted down and now, snug in the towel, he was his usual docile self. But Henry knew they were busted. Dejectedly, he twisted the lock, and swung open the door.

His mom surveyed the scene in stunned silence. Henry had the good sense not to say a word. She took note of the water dripping down the walls, the muddy-looking bathwater still streaking the tub, the shampoo that had spilled all over the floor, and the fact that one of her best towels now contained a dog.

It was Lucky who took matters into his own hands. Leaping out of Henry's grasp, he ran over and, with the exquisite timing of a master showman, began gently licking Mary's bare foot. To Henry's utter amazement, his mother burst out laughing.

CHAPTER 8

They agreed not to discuss a thing until they had cleaned up the bathroom and had breakfast. Henry and his mom set to work cleaning the tiles and the bathtub and the floor, but it did not escape Henry's notice that his mom let Lucky stay right there while they worked.

When they finally finished all the cleaning and were down in the kitchen, and after his mom had a very strong cup of coffee, they made their usual Saturday morning pancakes. They sat in silence as they ate the fluffy cakes, smothered with butter and syrup, while Lucky looked on, perfectly quiet and well behaved.

Mary poured another cup of coffee and turned to her son. "Henry, what is going on around here, and what is this – she turned to look at Lucky who appeared to be dozing after his strenuous bout with the bathtub – dog, doing in our house?"

This was not the way that Henry had envisioned introducing Lucky to his mom but he plunged ahead. He explained how he had found the little dog trapped in a hole and how, much as

26

wanted to keep him, he feared that it would just cost too much money, so he hid him while he tried to think of a plan. He admitted he had been sneaking outside when his mom came home last night, not to look at stars, but just to check on Lucky.

He was surprised when his mom interrupted him.

"Lucky?" she asked incredulously. "You named him Lucky?"

Well, this is an easy one, Henry thought. "Sure Mom, I named him Lucky because he was lucky that I rescued him from that hole and…." Henry paused as if realizing the truth of his next statement for the first time himself, "And I was lucky to have finally found a friend."

His mom was taken aback. After all that had happened to them in the past few months she had come to believe that nothing good or lucky would ever happen to them again. She knew how hard the move had been on Henry, so soon after losing his dad, and she had suspected he was having a hard time making friends. Now here he was, finding this little dog and giving him the most optimistic of names, because he still believed that lucky things could happen.

Tears began to smart behind her eyes and to hide her emotion she knelt down and scratched Lucky under his chin.

Henry took this as a very positive sign and was just starting to describe how he might be able to find some odd jobs in the neighborhood to help pay for Lucky's upkeep when his mom interrupted him yet again.

"No, Henry, don't worry about finding jobs. I think we're all lucky to have this new member of our family and we can afford him. Now, what do you say we get dressed and go to the store. We have to get Lucky some proper food, a collar, a leash, and…." She didn't have a chance to finish her sentence because Henry and Lucky were already excitedly racing out of the kitchen. Before she even had a chance to take another sip of coffee Henry was back. He gave her a big hug. "Thanks, Mom!"

She felt her spirits lift as she watched Henry tear happily out of the kitchen again. It was the most animated she had seen him since they had moved to this new town.

And I'm lucky too, she thought to herself as she mentally calculated the cost of a dog, which would surely be a stretch for their budget, that he found a beagle instead of a Great Dane!"

CHAPTER 9

They had fun buying Lucky's collar and having his name engraved on the pewter tag along with their phone number in case he ever got lost, a happenstance Henry refused to even imagine. Henry noticed that his mom would only buy the best dog food for Lucky, even though it was more expensive than a number of the cheaper bags. She had obviously done a little research online herself.

And then, to Henry's astonishment, they actually stopped for lunch at a little café in the heart of town. "Do we have enough money to do this?" Henry whispered as they were seated. And his mom, looking as pleased as he had seen her since they had moved said, "Yes we do. Just for this one lucky day. Order anything you want."

And Henry did.

The rest of the weekend passed in a pleasant blur. After some discussion it was agreed that Lucky could sleep in Henry's room, though on his own cozy newly purchased pad set right next to Henry's bed. With winter coming Henry really didn't have much trouble convincing his mom that it was only sensible to keep Lucky comfortable and safe indoors.

Henry spent much of Sunday trying to teach Lucky to shake hands and to roll over. Neither of these simple tricks managed to make their way onto the dog's radar screen, but Lucky didn't need any coaching to do the one thing that came naturally to him – snuggling up to Henry or his mom every chance he got.

The only damper on Henry's otherwise perfect weekend came as they were having dinner in the kitchen.

"You know, Henry," his mother said, "I saw the notice from school about the "Parent/Child Dinner." I was thinking of inviting your Uncle Roger to come visit and take you to that dinner. He is your father's brother, after all.

Henry nearly choked on his string beans. Oh, no, he thought to himself, not Uncle Roger! He actually had to take a couple of sips of water before he could respond. He wanted to choose his words carefully but this was simply a horrible idea!

"Mom," he said, "it's a parent-child dinner and you're my parent. I think I should go with you."

"That's sweet of you, Henry, but you and I will have many other opportunities. Your Uncle Roger calls every few days to check on us, and I know it would mean a lot to him to go to that dinner with you."

Henry knew better than to argue further, but his mind was racing. "Where is Uncle Roger at the moment?" he asked. If there was one constant in his uncle's life, it was that he never stayed in one place very long.

"Well," his mom replied, "when I spoke to him last he was in Arizona living on a Hopi Indian reservation. But he said he was nearly finished there and would be heading back east, so the timing for this dinner is likely to be perfect."

Henry sighed. It was going to take some doing to short circuit this disastrous plan.

CHAPTER 10

As he walked to school the next day, Henry pondered his dilemma. To be honest, he didn't really want to go to the school dinner at all, even with his mom, because he hated for her to discover he didn't have any friends. Who would they even sit with? But having Uncle Roger attend the dinner with him changed the equation entirely.

It was kind of hard to believe that his dad and Uncle Roger were really brothers. His dad had been a slight man, of medium height with a quiet, almost shy, demeanor. Uncle Roger was the polar opposite. Over six feet tall, with a flaming red beard, and a booming voice, Roger could – and would – talk to anyone, whether he knew them or not. Not only that, but you could never be sure what Roger would be wearing. Henry hadn't ever seen his uncle in a tie or a sport coat and doubted that he owned either one. Having just come from living with the Hopis, Roger could very well turn up at the school dinner in full Indian ceremonial dress. Henry shook his head. Once the kids at school got a load of Uncle Roger, they would never stop teasing him.

Henry slowed his pace as he approached the schoolyard. He wasn't anxious to start feeling the lonely isolation that settled over him every Monday morning, but there was no avoiding it. He reminded himself to continue his plan to be aloof and act like he just didn't care about anyone. The thought of the faithful Lucky, waiting for him at home, served to strengthen his resolve. He squared his shoulders, adjusted his bulging backpack, and strode through the school gate. He didn't need any of these dumb kids to be his friends; he had Lucky, and that was enough.

CHAPTER 11

Emily had chosen her outfit with special care this Monday morning. For the past couple of weeks she had been very busy, both before and after school, working on the school newspaper. But now the quarterly edition had been put to bed and she could get back onto a regular schedule. A schedule that she hoped might include seeing more of a certain Henry Caldwell. Not, of course, that she like-liked Henry, as she had hastened to explain to her best friend, Penelope, when they talked on the phone over the weekend. It was simply that she liked Henry, just as a friend. What could be simpler than that?

Emily had not forgotten their first, and only, meeting in front of Henry's locker the day of the fish incident. Despite that inauspicious beginning, she had often thought of Henry, recalling how nice he had seemed. She had even looked for him a few times, making a deliberate effort to pass his locker in hopes of running into him, but with no luck. Today, she vowed, would be different. Today she would find Henry. And, she had decided that morning as she also recalled that Henry was actually kind of cute, there was no reason not to look her best while she was at it. She smoothed the front of her favorite jumper and, feeling her usual pleasure at returning to school after the weekend, walked happily through the doorway.

CHAPTER 12

By lunchtime, Henry had to admit that he was doing a bang-up job of ignoring everyone, a task made particularly easy by the fact that everyone, as usual, was also ignoring him. As he sat alone in the lunchroom, listening to the noisy throng surrounding him, he couldn't help but feel sorry for himself. And this, he thought, is exactly how the parent-child dinner is going to be. Just Uncle Roger and me, sitting all by ourselves, and that's the best-case scenario. Uncle Roger had never known a stranger, so he would be sure to horn his way into sitting at a table with some poor unsuspecting parent and child, who would soon be wondering what had hit them.

The smell of pizza drifted across the room, fresh from the big cafeteria ovens, making Henry's mouth water. He looked down at his own lunch, which he always brought from home to save money. A baloney sandwich, an apple, and he noticed, brightening, a few of his mom's homemade cookies. It's cheaper to make our own cookies than buy them, she had explained as she beat the flour and creamed butter together, with the chocolate chips sitting at the ready. Henry smiled to himself as he bit into the rich, chewy cookie – one of the perks of being poor!

As usual, the last class of the day dragged by interminably for Henry, and not just because it was math. Spending all his time acting like he didn't care about anyone had taken its toll, and by day's end Henry was tense and irritable. He raced to his locker the minute the final bell rang and was so intent on hurriedly stuffing the books he would need for homework into his backpack that he didn't even notice Emily's arrival.

She stood silently for a minute, watching Henry's single-minded work, not wanting to interrupt. Then, as he began to pull the clasps on his pack closed, Emily gently touched his shoulder. Henry started in surprise, turning to face her.

Emily smiled. "Hi Henry," she said feeling suddenly shy, "I was kind of hoping to run into you today."

Henry glanced at her, betraying barely a trace of recognition. "Oh, yeah, sure, hi," he said coldly, before turning back to secure the final cinch on his backpack.

Emily wasn't quite sure what to do next. For some reason, as she could plainly see, Henry didn't want to have anything to do with her. She could not imagine why, but her feelings were already hurt enough to make her want to get out of this awkward situation as quickly as possible.

Henry immediately saw the hurt and embarrassment in Emily's eyes, and his first instinct was to apologize. But then he remembered his vow to ignore everyone in school, and that included Emily Stone. Why should he be the only person who was miserable around here? He hefted his backpack onto his shoulder, locked his locker and said dismissively, "Gotta go." And he strode off, leaving Emily standing by herself.

Emily walked slowly back to her own locker. She hadn't expected such a cold reception and she actually felt near tears from sheer embarrassment. But the more she thought about it, the more her emotion changed from hurt to anger. There would be no tears shed for Henry Caldwell, she concluded with a clench of her jaw. She couldn't believe how much she had misjudged him. "What a jerk he is," she decided.

Emily wasn't alone in that assessment. What a jerk I am, Henry thought to himself as he walked home, his spirits at a new low. He kept seeing the surprise and hurt on Emily's face when he responded to her so rudely, and suddenly this being aloof thing didn't really seem like such a cool idea. He knew deep down that Emily was only trying to be nice to him, something no one else had done, and now he was kicking himself for ruining his one chance to actually have a friend at school. He kept hearing her words over and over in his head – I kind of hoped to run into you today. No one had said such a welcoming thing to him since he had come to this new school, and look how he had replied. He shook his head in disgust.

Henry no sooner opened the front door than Lucky came speeding around the corner ready to greet him. Henry sat on the floor and hugged the little dog. Usually he would give Lucky a full rundown on what had happened at school, but today he couldn't bring himself to say a word. He was too ashamed to tell Lucky how he had treated Emily and he knew darned well that Lucky, who was always so loyal and kind, would not have approved at all.

CHAPTER 13

It didn't take long for Henry's gloom to be compounded. His mom returned home from work in high spirits and she lost no time in sharing her good news.

"Henry, have I got a wonderful surprise for you," she said as they sat in the kitchen waiting for the meatloaf to come out of the oven, the mashed potatoes and green beans already on the table. "Your Uncle Roger called today to say that he'll be here a whole week earlier than he had planned. He arrives this coming Saturday. Isn't that great?"

It was a measure of the depth of Henry's dismay that, despite the prospect of his favorite dinner, he instantly lost his appetite.

"Well, I mean, wow, that is a surprise," he said trying not to sound as disappointed as he felt. But then he had a glimmer of hope – if Uncle Roger was coming early maybe he was also leaving early. "Does this mean that Uncle Roger is going to have to leave before the parent/child dinner?" he asked, trying not to sound too hopeful.

"Of course not, honey," his mom replied as she sliced the meat loaf. Your Uncle Roger said he can't wait to meet all your new friends. He wouldn't miss the dinner for the world, so you don't have to worry about that."

Henry picked glumly at his meal.

Oh, but I do have to worry about that, he thought to himself, considering that I don't HAVE any friends for Uncle Roger to meet. Which made him think of how many other things he didn't have anymore which, if anyone happened to be keeping track, included not only the greatest loss, his dad, but also his old house, his old friends, his beloved fencing – he stopped counting as the list seemed endless. Which, for some reason, made him think of Emily again and how badly he had treated her. How, he wondered, had his life gotten to be such a mess?

Later that evening, wearing a sweater against the evening chill, Henry took Lucky out for their final walk of the day. Lucky bounded along with his usual enthusiasm, treating every tree, every acorn, every blade of grass as if he were discovering it for the first time. Henry, still too ashamed to confide in Lucky about his rudeness to Emily, figured he might as well at least give the little dog a heads up about the typhoon that was Roger Caldwell that was inexorably bearing down on their quiet household.

"See, Lucky, the thing about Uncle Roger is that he's like a force of nature. He never does anything quietly. It's surprising he and my dad were so close; gosh I remember how much they used to go hunting and fishing together. What an unlikely pair they were." Henry paused to think. "Actually, Uncle Roger is impossible to describe. But, what you need to realize, Lucky, is that once he arrives at our house things are not going to be the same."

Lucky, ever the optimist, continued his energetic wanderings. He did not appear to share Henry's concern in the least.

CHAPTER 14

Henry hit the snooze button one more time and burrowed deeper under the covers trying, as he always did, to keep the school day at bay for at least 10 more minutes at a time. On this particular morning, though, Henry had yet another reason to dread going to school – he hated the thought of running into Emily. If anything, his embarrassment about his inexcusably rude behavior had actually increased overnight and he knew that he would feel like a complete fool in her presence. And rightfully so, he admitted to himself.

But, whether by sheer luck on his part, or design on Emily's part, their paths did not cross for the rest of the week. By Friday the sharp edge of his shame had dulled enough that Henry was no longer looking over his shoulder to see if Emily was just around the corner. Besides, he had enough to worry about, what with Uncle Roger about to arrive the next day.

So, of course, just as his guard was down, he turned a corner and there was Emily. Not that he noticed her right away. She wasn't paying much attention either so they actually collided into each other. Emily's books, which she was carrying in her arms, scattered all over the floor.

Henry felt a genuine stab of hurt when he saw how Emily instantly recoiled when she realized that the person she had run into was, of all people, Henry. But beyond that emotion, this encounter instantly brought back two more things to Henry: his shame at how badly he had treated her and his innate sense of decency. No longer trying to be the cool aloof person that he was already sick of, Henry knelt and gathered Emily's books.

Still kneeling, but before handing the books over to her he looked up said, "Emily, I want to say I'm sorry for how…um… dumb… I acted last week. I really WAS glad to see you, too, and I was just……," he paused trying to think how to put a good spin on it, but there was no good way to gloss over his rudeness and what the heck, he thought, just be honest. "I was acting like a jerk because I was lonely and I took it out on you. I'm really sorry," he said, immediately considering this a less than brilliant ending for something that suddenly was very important to him.

Emily was quiet for a moment. There was no doubt she had liked him from the minute she met him that fateful day when he discovered the fish in his locker, and he had certainly hurt her feelings with his crude brush off after she had gone to the effort of seeking him out. But Emily had the gift of being naturally empathetic, with an instinctive ability to appreciate how someone else might be feeling. But before she could respond, they were interrupted by a harsh chorus of laughter.

And there was Colby, accompanied by his usual entourage of fawning football players. Colby could not hide his glee, delighted at catching Henry on one knee in front of Emily, as if he were proposing.

"Now look, you crazy kids," Colby said solemnly, "don't you think you should wait at least until you graduate high school to get married?" The players around him exploded in laughter, some suggesting waiting "at least until junior year."

Emily blushed a deep crimson as Henry leapt to his feet. He was about to explain that this was not at all what it seemed when Colby, ever the manipulator, suddenly took a different tack.

Colby put his arm around Henry and gave him a friendly pat on the shoulder. "Hey, buddy," he said warmly, "we're just kiddin' you because we like you. We know you wouldn't propose marriage to the dopiest, geekiest girl in the school."

For a second, Colby's hurtful words about Emily didn't really register with Henry. All Henry felt was the arm around his shoulder, and all he heard was "because we like you." Was it possible that Colby Crane, the best athlete in the school, really did like him? And how easy it would be for Henry to make a flip remark at Emily's expense just to make these guys laugh and realize that he was, in fact, a very cool guy.

And he just might have done that had he not, right then, looked over at Emily and seen that her face was a study in embarrassment and pain – exactly as his had been so many other times thanks to Colby's taunts.

Henry shook his head, mostly in disgust at himself for even being tempted to do such a thing as deserting Emily. He shrugged out from under Colby's arm.

"Now I know why you have that "C" on your shirt, Colby," Henry said, moving closer to Emily. "It stands for coward, because only a coward would pick on a girl for no reason at all – especially a girl who is" … Henry paused but at this point he was just going with his heart…. "who is not only NOT a geek but is actually brilliant…and… he finished with something of a flourish… beautiful." And to make his point even more forcefully, he gave Colby a shove, sending him stumbling backward a few feet. The gang of players fell silent.

Colby flinched at Henry's words and actually looked down at the "C" on his shirt for a brief second, as if it might actually say "Coward." The shove from Henry came as a surprise, but as Colby started menacingly toward Henry to avenge this unheard of assault by a complete nobody pipsqueak, Colby's

46

teammates, who had clearly not liked Colby's insult to Emily, held him back.

"C'mon Colb," one of the enormous lineman said as he held Colby's arm and dragged him backward, "this really isn't worth it."

Colby, an accomplished bully who knew instinctively when he had lost his audience, backed off. This was obviously a battle he would not win, at least not this day. He glared at Henry but before walking off he threw a final warning, "You have not seen the last of this, Caldwell."

Henry glared right back, secretly amazed that he was still in one piece. He was smart enough to say nothing.

Emily and Henry stood silently for a few seconds after the football players left, each rather stunned, but for different reasons. Emily, initially terribly hurt by Colby's comments, was more than a little impressed by Henry's spirited defense in her behalf. And Henry, still in shock that the team hadn't torn him to pieces after he called Colby a coward, was suddenly feeling embarrassed at his public declaration about Emily's brains and beauty.

He needn't have worried. Emily spoke first. "Henry, that was…. I mean, you were… you were very brave and I won't forget what you did." She paused and then asked with a self-

47

conscious laugh, "Do you really think I'm beautiful and brilliant?"

And for once Henry, pushing his glasses that always slipped down his nose back into place, didn't need to think about what to say or worry about what anyone might think. "I do," he said with a grin that was as genuine as any he had felt since coming to this new school. "I absolutely do."

CHAPTER 15

Henry flew home, his feet barely hitting the ground. Could this have been a better day? Henry thought to himself, almost in disbelief. He mulled over every aspect of the encounter with Colby and his gang, but he always ended up focusing solely on Emily's words, "You were very brave."

Yes!! This was something Lucky really needed to hear about and Henry could not wait to get home and tell him he had finally stood up to Colby and was, by the way, considered *very brave* by the brilliant not to mention, beautiful, Emily Stone. The fact that Lucky had not been informed about Henry's recent lapses did not trouble Henry at all – it was time for some good news for the Caldwell household and Henry was about to deliver it.

CHAPTER 16

Henry plowed through the front door of his house happier than he had been in months, and then came to a sudden halt. Something was different. He could just feel it.

Lucky, who always greeted him when he came home, was nowhere to be seen. And there was a strangely electric vibe in the house. Henry could hear conversations and laughter coming from the kitchen and he noticed the smell of something very unusual cooking. He dropped his backpack and with his spirits drooping, slumped against the door. This could only mean one thing.

Uncle Roger had arrived.

And, as was so typical of his completely unpredictable uncle, Roger had arrived an entire day earlier than expected.

Henry steadied himself for the worst and walked into the kitchen.

What a scene it was. His mom, who had gotten home early, was cooking some strange concoction under Roger's loud and, at least it seemed to her, hilarious direction. Worse, Lucky was sitting in Roger's lap, so completely hypnotized by Roger's gentle stroking that he didn't even notice Henry had arrived home.

But, taking no notice of Henry's apprehension, Uncle Roger reacted to his nephew's arrival with his unfailing exuberance. He rose from his chair, and setting the drowsy Lucky carefully onto the floor, engulfed Henry in a crushing hug. Henry was astounded by his uncle's strength and enthusiasm - and truthfully it did feel good to be greeted in such a genuinely warm way. He found himself basking in the comfort of this great bear hug and in his Uncle Roger's traditional greeting. "Henry," Roger said as always, "I love you."

It would have been nice if Henry could have responded in kind, but except to his mom, saying the words *I love you* did not come easily to him.

So he settled for a lukewarm, "Gee, it's nice to see you, too, Uncle Roger." This pallid greeting did not seem to bother his uncle one single bit. Roger settled happily back into his chair, looking as at home as if he had been born in that very spot, and then instantly disarmed his nephew with his next comment. "Henry," he said pointing at Lucky, "this is the best dog I've ever seen, bar none."

"Come over here and look at this," his mother commanded, beckoning to Henry with her wooden spoon. She directed his attention to the contents of a large pot. "Have you ever seen anything like it?" And indeed Henry had not, which was not surprising because this was an authentic Hopi Indian recipe which Uncle Roger declared was one of his all-time favorites. The Hopi corn stew bubbled gently on the stove, melding the flavors of beef, potatoes, carrots, and hominy, the puffed corn kernels that Henry had never seen, let alone tasted. Seasoned with the various spices Uncle Roger had brought straight from the Arizona reservation in small, unmarked leather bags, it was a mouth-watering combination.

"Now, of course the Hopis would be more likely to use buffalo or venison instead of ground beef," Uncle Roger explained as he joined them at the stove to oversee the cooking of his fry bread. He placed dough into hot oil and, in his inimitable way, roared his approval when the patties puffed and browned. "This is actually a Navajo recipe," he said with a wink as he placed the piping hot bread onto paper towels to drain, "but I don't think the Navajos would object if we pair their fry bread with Hopi stew!"

The stew was delicious, Henry had to admit. And he was quite sure he would be happy to eat fry bread every day of the week from now on. During dinner, Uncle Roger regaled them with tales of his adventures with the Hopis and, despite his earlier misgivings, Henry found himself actually having fun, drawn in by his uncle's fascinating stories punctuated by

Roger's boisterous, infectious laughter as he turned the jokes on himself.

So, it was not surprising that Henry's guard was completely down when Uncle Roger switched gears. "Henry, my boy," said Uncle Roger, "do you know what one of the most famous Hopi sayings of all time is?" Henry was taken aback, feeling at first as if somehow he should know the most famous Hopi saying of all time, which of course he did not, since until this evening he had not really been aware of the Hopi Indians at all, let alone their sayings. But he could tell in the next instant, from the twinkle in his uncle's eye, that it was rhetorical question, one his uncle did not expect him to know the answer to. So, after a quick swallow of the (regretfully) last of his fry bread he said simply, "No, Uncle Roger, I don't," and settled in, expecting another funny story.

Roger leaned back in his chair, having somehow magically managed to finish two helpings of dinner despite talking nonstop the entire time. He wasted no time with the answer.

"The Hopis say: 'The Creator has made the world; come and see it.'"

And in the brief silence that followed, Uncle Roger completely blindsided Henry.

"So, how about you call up some of your friends this evening and invite them to join us, because tomorrow we are going on a hike to see the world that the Creator made. There are some very interesting things to explore in this part of this country. It will be a great experience, but it will only be special if we share it with others."

Henry felt as if he had been hit by a truck. How could a dinner that was so much fun just a minute ago turn into such a disaster? Should he just tell Uncle Roger the truth?

Wonder how this would fly, he thought to himself as he ran over possible replies such as, "Well, Uncle Roger, that's not such a great idea because for starters, I actually don't have any friends."

But, as it turned out, he didn't have to respond right away because, as usual, Uncle Roger retained the floor, continuing on with his nonstop thoughts. "I know just the place for us to hike and we will make some wonderful discoveries. This is going to be fantastic!" And then Uncle Roger moved on to other topics as if this one thing was completely settled – tomorrow he and Henry and Henry's vast network of friends would be off on their adventure.

Henry, feeling panicky, looked over at his mom for a little support, but she had apparently forgotten any concerns she once had about his lack of friends. She must have fallen under

Roger's spell because she started clearing the dishes and, instead of helping, she made things worse. "Henry, Roger and I will take care of the dishes. You go off and call your friends."

Riiiight, Henry thought as he walked out of the kitchen. Why don't I just go right on out and call my many friends to come over tomorrow and take a hike with my crazy Uncle Roger? As he left the kitchen, Henry called to Lucky, but Lucky had taken up residence in Uncle Roger's lap and appeared to be asleep under Rogers's rhythmic petting. Thanks a lot, pal, Henry thought, as he walked out of the kitchen feeling very alone.

CHAPTER 17

To give Lucky his due, he turned up just a few minutes later, nuzzling close to Henry, who was sitting in the living room trying to think of what to do next. It meant a lot to have Lucky there. Henry lifted the little dog into his lap and, as they had done so many times before, they engaged in their version of conversation – Henry talking, Lucky listening.

"Okay, Lucky, here's where we are. I didn't have a chance to tell you earlier, but I actually had a good…well, actually a *great*… day at school today with Emily." Lucky didn't seem to get it and Henry realized he had not told Lucky much about Emily, since until today most of their past history did not showcase Henry's finest moments.

"Anyway," Henry continued speaking softly to Lucky, "here's the thing. For reasons unknown to you, Emily thinks I'm (and here Henry could not help but experience again the best feeling ever)…well… very brave." He looked at the equally brave little pup that had come through so much. "What do you think, Lucky, should I call her and ask her to come hike with us tomorrow?" Henry paused, and then added something he would only say to Lucky. "She's actually the only friend

56

I've got." Lucky wagged his tail so enthusiastically that Henry took this as a definite yes, even though Lucky always wagged his tail the exact same way, no matter what Henry said.

Henry did not have a cell phone, which put him in a minority of one at school. He had one before his dad died, but after that a cell phone was too expensive to maintain. It was a wrench to give it up at first, but soon enough he had such a long list of more serious losses he had really not given the lack of the phone much thought.

He would have loved to text Emily, but since that was impossible he had no choice but to pick up the landline. He looked up Emily's home telephone number in the school directory and his hand shook as he punched in each individual digit. He hesitated over the last one, and then made the decision to go ahead and simply do it. He pushed the last button and crossed his fingers. Please, please, let it be Emily who answers the phone.

"Hello," said a gruff voice, most emphatically not Emily. Just my luck, thought Henry, who for a split second considered hanging up. But he hadn't come this far to turn back now. He took a deep breath and, recalling his mother's never-ending insistence on good phone manners said, "Hello, this is Henry Caldwell, a friend of Emily's from school. May I speak to her, please?"

Elliot Stone was actually impressed by a kid who could speak in courteous sentences. And who, to his amazement, actually used the telephone! His stern tone softened slightly. "You want to speak to my daughter, Emily, do you?" he asked. "Yes sir," said Henry, adding for good measure, "but not for long, only a couple of minutes."

Seconds later Emily was on the line. "Hi Henry," she said casually, as if a call from Henry Caldwell was the most natural thing in the world. Then she added, "It's great to hear from you."

Those few kind words made Henry feel suddenly confident. When he heard 'It's great to hear from you' his nervousness seeped instantly away. He wished Lucky could have heard those words, just to prove to him that his emphatic tail wagging had been right on the mark! But, there was no time for that right now.

Henry took a deep breath. "Thanks, Emily, it's great to talk to you, too," he said as he gathered his courage to invite her to.......well, with Uncle Roger at the helm, to heaven knows what. But this was no time for wobbling; he wanted this to sound like a really fun invitation.

"So, my Uncle Roger just arrived in town today for a visit, fresh from working on a Hopi Indian reservation in Arizona." Emily was silent – understandably figured Henry who briefly wondered why he couldn't have an uncle who was more…normal. He shook those thoughts off and continued. "Tomorrow he would like to take me and some friends on a hike to show us some really interesting things and I….. was….. well….I was thinking….." He couldn't get another word out.

Emily saved him. "Gee, that sounds great. I'd love to come but I have to babysit my little brother, Eddie, tomorrow." Henry's spirits sank.

But Emily wasn't done. She continued, "Eddie is nearly nine and he loves to hike. Any chance he could come along? If so, we'd love to join you." Henry's spirits soared! He could actually produce *two* friends for the hike. Friends, of course, was a somewhat relative term since he barely knew Emily and had never met Eddie, but so what. They settled on the details – Henry and Uncle Roger would pick them up at their house at 10 a.m. Exhilarated, Henry hung up the phone and sat for a minute in silent amazement. As recently as this morning, he realized, this phone call would have been impossible.

CHAPTER 18

Henry awoke early, too excited about the hike to sleep a minute longer. Actually, he was more excited about spending the day with Emily, but still, he felt like the whole day held promise and looking forward to a day that held promise was something he hadn't experienced in a long time.

He could tell from the sounds floating up from the kitchen that he was not the earliest riser this Saturday morning. His uncle's booming laugh was already reverberating through the house and the smell of breakfast cooking provided a big incentive to finish dressing in a hurry and get downstairs. Lucky, quivering in anticipation at the prospect of an earlier than usual walk, bounded back and forth between Henry and the doorway, as if that would somehow hasten things along.

Henry and Lucky returned from their walk to find the scene in the kitchen exactly the kind of chaos that always seemed to surround Uncle Roger. Bacon was sizzling in a cast iron skillet, his mother was pouring strong, aromatic coffee brewed to Uncle Roger's exacting specifications into two stout mugs, and sandwiches were being prepared for what Uncle Roger typically declared would be "the world's greatest picnic."

Roger himself was the picture of an outdoorsman, wearing well-worn hiking boots, a soft, plaid flannel shirt, a khaki vest with more pockets than Henry had ever seen, and a bright red kerchief around his neck that somehow, on Roger, instead of clashing with his bushy red beard, actually looked dashing. He was, as usual, in the process of doing multiple things at once – packing a knapsack with water bottles, wrapping the sandwiches, counting out enough apples for everyone, and somehow at the same time effortlessly managing to scramble a half dozen eggs to perfection.

Henry tucked into his bacon and eggs, enjoying the unusual sense of bustle and purpose that swirled around him. His mom, looking relaxed and happy, was making plans to take Lucky on a good long walk later in the day, since Uncle Roger had announced that the hike he had in mind would be too strenuous for the little dog.

Henry finished his breakfast and carried his plate to the sink. In some distant corner of his mind Henry realized that, at least for this one day, things were somehow better thanks to Uncle Roger. But he also found himself reserving judgment – nothing was ever predictable when Uncle Roger was in the mix and the Parent/Child Dinner was still looming. But, on this particular Saturday morning, it was so pleasant not to be all alone wondering what to do with himself that he just let his misgivings about his uncle melt away.

CHAPTER 19

Emily and Eddie were waiting right out in front of their neat ranch-style house, which was in the next development over from Henry's. Henry made a mental note about how easy it would be to take Lucky for a walk and just happen, by sheer coincidence, to end up right in front of Emily's house.

Uncle Roger leapt from the car to greet his two new best friends, which was the way he always felt about everyone, even those he had just met. Henry was worried that Emily and Eddie might be put off by Uncle Roger's effusive greeting, but it seemed to be just the opposite. They obviously felt instantly at home with the tall, bearded man whose idea of hello was to give them each a crushing two-handed handshake that seemed never to end while insisting they call him Uncle Roger.

Emily introduced Eddie to Henry. Henry, unlike his ebullient uncle, could think of nothing more exciting than to shake Eddie's hand with only one hand and say that it was nice to meet him. Eddie was small for his age but he was blessed with an outgoing personality, which endeared him to Uncle Roger instantly. Eddie was invited to sit up front and he and Roger were soon engaged in a nonstop conversation.

This arrangement could not have suited Henry more, as Emily was relegated to the back seat, right next to him. But, as Eddie and Roger jabbered on, Henry was dismayed to find that he suddenly could not think of a single interesting thing to say. He wracked his brain to no discernable effect. He finally settled on the most banal comment, "Gosh, what a great day for a hike." Brilliant, Henry, he thought to himself the minute the words tumbled out of his mouth, what fascinating thing are you going to say next, "How's the weather?"

But the irrepressible Eddie saved the day, suddenly turning in his seat to ask Henry, out of the clear blue, "Do you really have a sword? Emily said so."

It took Henry a moment to figure out what Eddie meant, but then he realized that Emily must have told Eddie that he fenced. The thought that she remembered his fencing delighted him no end. He grinned and said, "I sure do Eddie." And this time he didn't fumble the ball. "Maybe Emily will bring you over to my house sometime soon and I can show it to you," he added, rather pleased to see that Emily was nodding in agreement.

CHAPTER 20

They arrived at the trailhead and parked in the nearby parking lot, which was not even half full this early on a chilly fall morning.

Uncle Roger shrugged his food-laden knapsack onto his broad shoulders and led them along a short wooded trail and across a bridge to the beginning of what was known as "The Bighorn Trail." Before they set off on their official hike, Uncle Roger pulled them together for a talk.

He started off with a question. "We are about to climb the Bighorn Trail. Who knows anything about the Bighorn sheep, the namesake of this trail?" There was silence from his gang of climbers. No one knew much of anything about Bighorn sheep.

"Well," continued Uncle Roger, "bighorn sheep are mountain sheep that are able to climb through steep and rocky areas in the craggiest mountains. They get their name from their massive horns, which in the males are very big and curl down around their faces. I would not want to tangle with a male bighorn sheep, I can tell you that," Roger said with a shudder, "but I sure would like to be able to climb rocks like a bighorn. Today, what we are going to try to do is climb this Bighorn Trail as if we were bighorn sheep ourselves!"

Henry listened spellbound, as did Emily and Eddie. Were they really going to climb over rocks that required the skill of bighorn sheep? Surely there was not that kind of a climb this close to the city, thought Henry, even as he realized this trail was, after all, named for the Bighorns.

Henry found it interesting to see that his usually loud uncle was exactly the opposite out here in the natural setting that he loved and revered. His voice was quiet, and he radiated a respect for the beautiful surroundings. Uncle Roger's next words confirmed Henry's observations. "We are just visitors to this sacred place. We must leave it better than we found it," he said quietly.

Before they set off Roger explained to them that the trail they would follow had been blazed with yellow paint. "It will get confusing once we really get onto the trail, so we must always look for the yellow blaze that will lead us the right way." Roger paused, and then put his hand on Eddie's shoulder. "Eddie, I put you in charge of looking for the yellow blazes – you are the leader of the blaze."

Eddie did not hesitate for a single second. "I can do it, Uncle Roger," he said with a confidence that he did not completely feel. But there was something about Roger's belief in him that boosted his own belief in himself. If he were in charge of finding the yellow blaze, thought the nearly nine-year-old Eddie, delighted at his unexpected leadership role, he would find a way to do the job.

Roger paused and then brought his gang of three close to link their hands together, saying, "Let's go see this beautiful world." And with Eddie in the lead looking diligently for the yellow blaze on the next tree or a rock to steer their way, they set off.

CHAPTER 21

The trail, which was actually a very easy walk, led them through a pleasant forest. It was a snap to see the yellow blazes well ahead on trees, though no one wanted to tell Eddie that they already knew the route, as he took his job very seriously. So everyone acted as if they had NOT seen the yellow markers on so many trees ahead.

Henry felt let down. If this was Uncle Roger's idea of a hike, maybe his uncle should lower his sights and just take a bunch of 8-year-olds on walks because this hike was, there was no other way to put it, simply boring. As usual, Uncle Roger seemed unperturbed, encouraging Eddie to keep a sharp eye out for the next yellow blaze.

Great, thought Henry, who could see the next *three* yellow blazes ahead on their simple path, let's just waste our time strolling through the woods. Henry, as his uncle had directed, was bringing up the rear so the only positive was that he did have the pleasure of being near Emily as they negotiated the few minor bumps in the trail. But, to Henry's credit, he had enough insight to realize that his disappointment was rooted in

68

a strange turnabout. He had gone from not even wanting to go on this hike, to (once Emily had agreed to come) hoping that it would be something special, and the fact that it was not going to be special was suddenly one more disappointment in Henry's long list of disappointments over this past year.

Just as Henry was about to resign himself to the boredom of this truly nothing hike they came right up against – literally – a sheer rock wall. The only way forward was to climb up through a small walkway and true to form, Uncle Roger asked Eddie to lead the way, though Henry noticed this time his uncle stayed close behind his pint-sized leader. And Roger was concerned enough about this part of the walk to look back at Emily and Henry and caution, "Pay attention as you climb up here – we are about to start the real hike." By then, Eddie was almost out of sight, having clambered up the stone outcroppings at a rapid pace. Even before they reached the top they heard Eddie's exuberant shout when he saw what lay ahead.

CHAPTER 22

Having at last crested the top, what a sight it was. As Emily and Henry finally scaled the last of the walkway they were met with something they had not expected. Before them, stretching as far as they could see, was a vast expanse of huge boulders. It seemed impossible to even think about navigating such a rocky jumble on foot but then they heard the excited voice of the intrepid Eddie. "There's the yellow blaze," he yelled, pointing to a nearby rock off to the right. "Let's go!"

And go they did. They climbed over big rocks and slid down others, always on the lookout for Eddie's next yellow blaze to keep them on the track. Without that they would not have had a clue which way to go. He never failed them.

At one point they came to a ravine in the rocks that they had to jump over. Somehow Uncle Roger must have realized this was coming, because by then he was in the lead and when he saw how great the leap was, he simply reached out his arm to Eddie and easily hoisted him across. Henry, who witnessed this from his place last in the line, was in awe. His uncle had just stretched out his arm and swung the 60-pound Eddie across the

70

ravine as if he were nothing more than a five-pound sack of potatoes. Henry was still thinking about his uncle's strength when they reached the top of the rock climb. From this towering vantage point they could see the river below and the rocky ledges that lined the opposite shore. An occasional kayaker paddled by, heading to the rapids downstream. Henry was hot and his legs were aching. He no longer had any interest in complaining about how ridiculously easy this hike was!

Fortunately, at just this moment Uncle Roger spied a flat area that overlooked the river. He beckoned them to follow him and they all sat down gratefully, resting their backs against the rocks that had been warmed by the midday sun.

Uncle Roger, who seemed tireless, was the picture of efficiency, handing out bottles of water, sandwiches and apples. They ate ravenously, not having realized until now how hungry they were. It was an idyllic setting – the warm sun, the languid river far below, the wonderfully delicious water in the bottles and the sandwiches, which would have tasted ordinary at home, but here in this hard to reach spot that could only be attained by rigorous climbing, seemed extraordinary. No one spoke, not even the voluble Eddie or the ever-talkative Uncle Roger, and the silence seemed just right, almost respectful. When they had finished their meal, Uncle Roger distributed one of Henry's mom's homemade chocolate chip cookies to each of them.

They ate their cookies with gusto, careful not to let even a crumb of the delectable treats escape.

Under Roger's direction they were careful to gather all their bottles and paper wrappings to be sure they left this perfect picnic spot as pristine as they had found it. "Leave nothing but footprints," Uncle Roger cautioned. They even found a couple of other bottles that had been left behind by careless hikers, and they gathered those up too. They would leave this rocky picnic area even better than they found it. Roger packed all the trash in his knapsack, and then called them together.

"The next part of this trail will start downhill and will end at a small beach. When we get there, I have something very special to show you," he said.

"What is it?" asked Eddie, always curious and never shy about asking questions. But Uncle Roger put him off. "It's not something for words, Eddie," he replied, "it's something you have to experience. You'll see when we get there."

CHAPTER 23

Eddie continued to expertly spy the yellow blazes and they zigged and zagged across the rocks, always heading downward. At one point there was a narrow chute between the rocks and they all slid down as if on a giant granite sliding board.

At last they reached the small beach, now level with the river that had seemed so far away when they saw it from their perch on the high rocks where they had eaten lunch. Henry looked around. It was a nice place but nothing about it looked very unusual to him. He wondered what his uncle had in mind when he said he had something "very special" to show them.

He didn't have to wait long to find out.

Uncle Roger was already carefully scanning the many small rocks that had washed up along the shoreline. His shout brought them all running. When they arrived, Uncle Roger was rinsing a rock that he had found in the cold water that ran steadily downstream toward the falls. He gathered them close and showed them his find, which he held reverently in the palm of his hand.

73

"This is very special," he told them. "This," he paused, looking at it thoughtfully once again, "is a love rock."

They all stared in silence at the rock in Uncle Roger's hand. To their amazement, it was shaped almost exactly like a heart. But they had no idea what to make of it.

Not surprisingly, Eddie was the first to speak. "How did the rock get shaped like a heart?" he asked. The others had been wondering the same thing.

Uncle Roger spoke quietly. "It didn't happen just by accident, that's for sure," he told them, giving his heart rock a final rinse in the cold river. The sun reflecting off the droplets made it shimmer. "If water and wind could transform rocks into just anything, then we would find rocks in the shape of all sorts of things, like dogs, or trains or sailboats. But we don't. And yet we do find rocks in the shape of hearts. They're not always as perfectly shaped as this one," he added with a smile. "Very often the heart shape is not even obvious at first glance, but love rocks exist for those who seek them."

Roger held the heart-shaped rock up between his thumb and forefinger and continued. "The heart is a symbol of the greatest power there is - the power of love that is freely given. Love rocks are a reminder that love originates from a higher place, well beyond each one of us, and all we need to do is choose to pass it on."

74

"Now," said Uncle Roger, rousing his troops to action, "when you find a love rock, you are holding something that harnesses the power of love; when you give a love rock, you are unleashing that power." He turned the rock over once again in his hand. "What makes a love rock so valuable is that it is not man-made. It is something that no amount of money can ever buy."

He surveyed the tiny beach that was lapped by small waves driven by the current. He swung his arm expansively toward the little sandy outcropping covered in rocks. "To give a love rock, you must first find one. Go and look," he said to Eddie, Emily and Henry. "Love rocks are there for all who are willing to search."

They set to the task eagerly, each certain that he or she would find a rock as quickly as Uncle Roger had. But, as they discovered, it was not that easy. It was nearly 15 minutes later before Emily exclaimed, "I found one!" They all gathered round as she held out the rock for their inspection.

Henry hated to say it, but Emily's rock did not look at all like a heart to him. He hemmed and hawed a bit and then said, "Emily, I don't think that actually looks like a heart." Emily stared at him in disbelief. "Of course it does, Henry," she said handing the rock to him and urging him to turn it around so he could see that although it might not be perfect, it was still clearly heart-shaped. Henry tried his best, twisting and turning it in his hand, but he could never make out a heart shape at all.

They were interrupted by a whoop from Eddie. "I found one, too," he said, running over to show the group his love rock. Emily held it up and turned it over and over. "Eddie, this is beautiful," she said, giving him a high five. Just like Emily's rock it wasn't perfectly shaped, but it was a heart rock nonetheless. Emily turned to Henry. "You might not have liked my heart rock, but you sure can't argue with this one." Henry took Eddie's rock and looked it over carefully. It looked like a plain old rock to him, not a bit like a heart. But by now he was feeling like the odd man out and he didn't want to ruin everyone's fun. "Yes, of course," he said lying to one and all, "it sure does look like a heart."

Eddie and Emily showed their finds to Uncle Roger who smiled and said that their rocks were beautiful, and because they believed in them, they were filled with the power of love. The three friends spent the next half hour looking, but no one found another love rock.

Uncle Roger gave a shrill whistle and gathered them all back together. "Okay, gang, it's time to finish our hike and get everyone home safe and sound." And that is just what they did, with Eddie spotting the yellow blaze, and everyone following the rocky terrain until at last they came to the end. They walked easily along the creekside trail that led back to the car and soon they were in front of Eddie and Emily's house.

Emily made their thanks and she and Eddie said their farewells as they exited the car. But before they left, Eddie reached into his pocket. "Henry," he said, "take this. It was a really fun day." And he put his heart rock into Henry's hand.

Henry, who had been brooding on the way home about not having found a heart rock himself, was touched at the thoughtfulness of his little pal.

"Thanks, Eddie," he said, hoping he had mustered a genuine enough smile. He really did appreciate Eddie's gift, but it troubled him more than he could say that, for some reason, he could not see the heart shape in the rock Eddie had so generously given him. Nor had he been able to find a heart rock himself. Why, he asked himself, was such a simple thing so impossible for him?

Henry didn't mention a word of his dismay to Uncle Roger as they drove home. Of course, it would have been hard to get a word in edgewise or any other way for that matter as Uncle Roger talked exuberantly non-stop about the hike and how much he liked Emily and Eddie and heaven only knew what else. Henry barely heard a word, so lost was he in his own concerns. But after Uncle Roger parked the car and he and Henry started to gather their things, Uncle Roger said the strangest thing, seemingly out of nowhere, but somehow exactly to the point of Henry's doubts about his ability ever to see a love rock. "Don't worry, Henry," he counseled with an affectionate clap on Henry's shoulder, "you'll see it when you need to." He walked off before Henry had a chance to ask him another thing.

For the rest of the day Henry was busy with his weekend chores. He spent a good part of the afternoon raking leaves, composting them, and then working to clear a space for a garden. His mom, at Uncle Roger's urging, had agreed to plant some winter vegetables as yet another way to save money. Needless to say, Uncle Roger had no end of ideas about what "the absolutely most perfect vegetables" would be. In fact, Roger was so enthusiastic about the garden he had insisted on taking Henry's mom on a "purely exploratory" trip to the local nursery that very afternoon to see what was available.

Working in the cool fall air helped to clear Henry's mind. When he did think about the hike, he mostly recalled how much fun it was and how great it had been to be with Emily, and Eddie, too. He was close to convincing himself that the love rock part was the least important part of the day; that it made no difference at all whether he could find a rock shaped like a heart, of all crazy things. But, try as he might, and despite his uncle's counsel, he wasn't able to shake off a lingering disappointment at being the only one who just didn't seem to get it. It was bothering him enough that he vowed to talk this over with Lucky first chance he got.

CHAPTER 24

As it happened, Lucky and Henry never had that talk.

Uncle Roger and his mom arrived home laden with bags of topsoil, fertilizer, mulch and seedlings. Look at all this!" Henry's mother exclaimed. "Your uncle has bought us quite a garden, Henry." She pointed to the trays of seedlings. "Before we know it we'll be harvesting broccoli, onions and beets. Not to mention spinach and kale."

Not to mention spinach and kale would be just fine, Henry thought to himself, never having been a fan of either one of those greens, let alone beets and broccoli. But it was fun to see his mom's excitement about the garden, and Henry suddenly found himself wondering whether Uncle Roger's insistence that they go just to "explore" the nursery was borne of an intention to make sure that he was able to pay for all these things himself.

Roger was busy unloading the bags from the trunk, lifting them with such ease that Henry made a conscious decision not to offer to help. He hated the thought of his mom and Uncle

Roger seeing the extreme effort it would take for him to lift those 50-pound bags of soil and mulch. As usual, Roger was talking non-stop. "Henry, my boy, you've got a wonderful job cut out for you here, creating this magnificent garden. It will be a showplace, I have no doubt!"

Henry had plenty of doubt, having never planted a garden in his life, and certainly not one on this scale, but in some odd way he was looking forward to it. He was tired of having nothing much to do, especially since he could no longer fence, and he was ready to channel his energy into some productive physical activity.

He was still working on the garden when his mother came to the door. "Henry, you have a phone call," she said. It stopped Henry in his tracks. This, he realized, was the first time someone had called him since they had moved here.

He picked up the phone and was thrilled to find Emily on the other end of the line. They chatted amiably for a few minutes, with Henry describing the garden and the plans for a bounty of winter vegetables. He was so pleased to learn that Emily also harbored little enthusiasm for spinach and kale that he gave her a pass for liking beets.

"Please tell Uncle Roger how much Eddie and I enjoyed the hike today," Emily said. "Eddie has been talking about nothing else since we got home!" She paused, and then, sounding a bit hesitant, asked. "Are you by any chance going to the Parent/Child dinner next Saturday?" When Henry responded that he was, along with Uncle Roger, Emily's tone brightened. "Do you think you could, well, sit with my dad and me?"

Could we ever! Henry thought to himself, trying to dampen his enthusiasm. No point in coming across as the completely desperate person he actually was. "Well, sure...I guess..." But then his happiness got the best of him. "Of *course* we could," he replied with feeling. "That'd be great."

The rest of the day went by in a blur. Henry could not believe his good fortune. His dread of the Parent/Child dinner had instantly turned into eager anticipation – this might actually be fun! The sheer awfulness of arriving to a room full of strangers, having no place to sit, and looking like complete losers faded away into oblivion, making Henry realize just how much that worry, so suddenly vaporized, had been weighing on him.

Later that night, as he prepared for bed, he was still marveling at his reprieve. Lucky was right there, more than ready to settle into his own bed as he had spent a busy day outside racing around the garden plot. Henry held him close and gave him the awesome news, which Lucky took with his usual aplomb.

So great was Henry's relief about the dinner, he was suddenly no longer worried about the idea of finding – or in his case – not finding love rocks. He turned Eddie's rock over in his hand before dousing the lights. Sure enough, it still looked like nothing more than a common blob of stone – no heart shape to be seen. Henry shrugged and tossed the rock back onto his dresser. Life was definitely looking up and heart rocks were now the least of his worries. It didn't even occur to him to mention his earlier concerns about them to Lucky.

CHAPTER 25

At breakfast on Monday morning Uncle Roger announced, quite unexpectedly, that he had to leave for a few days to take care of some business. It was a sign of Henry's complete change of heart that he looked up worriedly from his pancakes and asked with genuine concern in his voice, "But will you be back in time for the dinner?"

Indeed he would, wouldn't miss it for the world, be back on Friday, Uncle Roger assured him in his usual tumble of words as he ambled out the door heading for, as Henry's mom noted with a shake of her head after he had left, "heaven knows where."

Henry stuffed his books into his backpack and topped it off with his lunch bag, which contained a ham and cheese sandwich that he was sure would not taste anywhere near as good as the exact same sandwich had at the top of the rock climb. He headed out after giving Lucky a final pat on the head, and walked to school with a lighter step than at any other time since he had arrived in this new town. Because now, thought Henry, I actually have friends at school.

Well, perhaps this was stretching it a bit. He calculated his number of friends at three: Emily, Eddie and Lucky. But Eddie went to a different school and Lucky was a dog, so to be completely accurate his friend count at his school was still pretty low – a total of one to be exact. But the power of having even one friend could not be denied. Henry approached the school gates without his usual sense of dismay for one simple reason – inside the building was someone who liked him.

Henry and Emily caught up between classes, but just for a few minutes. They had different schedules and unlike Henry, Emily was busy with after-school activities so they really didn't have much chance to talk. But just the fact that Emily made the effort to connect with him meant the world to Henry. For Emily, it presented a completely different issue – she once again had to emphatically assure Penelope that she absolutely did *not* like-like Henry Caldwell at all; he was just a friend, nothing more. But, as she spent more time around the lanky Henry, with his glasses perpetually slipping down his nose, and his unfailing sense of kindness, Emily wondered if her protestation was completely true.

For a day that had started off so well for Henry, it certainly ended on a sour note.

As he was packing up his books in front of his locker, who should appear but Colby and his ever present minions. It had been a while since the football players had time to hang out after school, but with the bigger games of the season coming up, they now had Monday afternoons off to rest up for the hard practices the rest of the week.

Colby was still seething from their last encounter when Henry had defended Emily by calling him a coward and he was glad to find Henry alone – Colby had learned his lesson about not making smart-aleck comments about girls, even one that he considered to be a complete dweeb.

"Well, if it isn't Zorro, the famous 'fencer,'" he said with his usual smirk, making a Z with his pretend air sword. "How's married life treating you, Caldwell?" The team laughed – they hadn't forgotten seeing Henry down on one knee in front of Emily as if he were proposing, which in their knucklehead world qualified as hilarity.

Henry was officially sick of this stuff. But, as usual, a clever retort eluded him.

Suddenly and without warning, Colby stepped forward and gave Henry forceful shove. Caught off guard, Henry landed heavily against the lockers. The players watched attentively to see what Henry would do next. Henry slowly straightened his glasses and instinctively rubbed his aching shoulder, which had absorbed the brunt of blow.

He honestly didn't get this. What was the pleasure in hurting someone?

"Why'd you do that, Colby?" he asked, genuinely bewildered by Colby's unprovoked violence. Henry could have sworn that a couple of the players looked like they might have been wondering the same thing, but if they were bothered by Colby's actions, none spoke up.

Colby smiled, but his smile held malice, not warmth.

"Just a preview of coming attractions, Caldwell," he said as he sauntered away, his teammates trailing obediently behind.

CHAPTER 26

Over the next three days Henry fell into a routine more agreeable than he ever could have imagined just a week before. With football practice in full swing he knew he wouldn't be the butt of any more of Colby's taunts, at least not until the team's day off next Monday. So Henry put that worry out of his mind and for the rest of the week he simply gave himself over to enjoying his walk to school on such unseasonably mild mornings for September, and the pleasant anticipation of seeing Emily each day. They had fallen into a routine of meeting, without fail, during the break before their 4th and 5th periods and it was the highlight of his day.

Each afternoon after he got home from school, as the sunlight paled and the air turned chill, he applied himself to the garden, always accompanied by the energetic Lucky, whose delight at spending extra hours outdoors knew no bounds. Henry looked forward to all these things, but most of all, he was looking forward to the Parent/Child dinner, and the chance to spend the entire evening with Emily.

The garden project was backbreaking work, requiring Henry to carefully remove the sod in long strips and replant it down by the shed where he had once hidden Lucky, to cover the unsightly brown areas of dead grass that had died before he and his mom had moved in. Then, using a pick ax to loosen the poor soil, Henry had to lift heavy chunks of red clay into a wheelbarrow and deposit them into the deep ravine running behind the house.

To his surprise, Henry found he actually liked the hard work. He enjoyed seeing the garden plot take shape and he could feel his muscles straining as he swung the heavy pick and hoisted the big hunks of clay. Each night he had to spend an extra few minutes in the shower to let the hot water calm his aching arms and back.

CHAPTER 27

Henry awoke Friday morning with a rare sense of excited anticipation. He was actually looking forward to his uncle's return, having discovered that he missed the kinetic energy that the perpetually-in-motion Roger invariably imparted to his surroundings. Of course, this was not to say that Henry didn't still have some concerns about what Uncle Roger might say or do when they got to the dinner tomorrow night. Roger loved a crowd, considering it to be a collection of people who would soon become his close friends, a worldview not always shared by the unsuspecting strangers that fell into his all-encompassing path. But, Henry hoped, Roger's effervescence would surely be neutralized by having Emily and her dad close at hand to soak up all that excess energy – and thank heavens for that.

From his bed Henry could see his clothes for tomorrow evening hanging on the closet door handle, all pressed and ready to go. His mom, ever the organizer, had insisted he try everything on. She had been shocked to see that his blue blazer was a bit tight across the shoulders and short in the sleeve. His shirt cuffs protruded much father beyond the blazer sleeves than she would have liked, and Mary quietly marveled at how much Henry had grown just in these last couple of months. But there was no time or money to be buying new blazers at this point, so his mom hit upon the only solution she could think of. "Henry," she had suggested, "be sure and wear a short sleeved shirt tomorrow night, okay?"

At school, each one of his 50-minute classes felt like 500 as the time dragged on interminably toward the best part of Henry's day, the break period when he would meet Emily. The time finally arrived in its own due course, not speeded up one single bit by how many times Henry checked his watch.

Henry arrived at their usual meeting spot first, having no doubt Emily would be there soon. For one thing, so far he had never known her to be late and besides, the midday break was only 15 minutes long so they really didn't have any time to waste. As he waited Henry watched the other kids enjoying their brief quarter hour respite from class. Most of them, of course, were on their phones or tablets, quite likely texting friends who were no more than a corridor away. Much as Henry wished he had this capability himself, he definitely preferred his in-person conversations with Emily. They both saved up interesting things to tell each other and Henry wondered if their daily meetings would be half as much fun if they had already texted their every thought to one another.

Henry glanced at his watch. Emily was already five minutes late – unheard of! He watched the second hand sweep relentlessly on as each of the remaining 10 minutes ticked away. He could not imagine what had happened, but then the bell rang and, with no other choice, he trudged reluctantly back to class.

Henry was jolted by the depth of his disappointment in not seeing Emily. His rational mind told him there could be any number of good reasons why Emily had not shown up – she might have had a meeting with a teacher or perhaps some crisis at the newspaper had come up, and of course since he didn't have a cell phone, she would have no way of letting him know. But the heart has a way of defying logical thinking, and Henry's heart was no different. He could not shake the growing feeling that Emily hadn't shown up for only one reason – because she had simply grown tired of him.

He hung around for a while after school, even nonchalantly (he hoped) strolling by Emily's locker a few times, but it was soon clear he wasn't going to run into her. So, Henry finally packed up his backpack and made his way home. There was far less spring in his step than when he had set off for school that morning.

CHAPTER 28

Henry unlocked the door and, despite all his misgivings, had to laugh as Lucky came skidding around the corner, barely able to contain his joy at seeing Henry. Here's one pal who isn't sick of me, Henry thought, kneeling to scratch Lucky in his favorite place, right behind the ears.

"Hang on a minute, bub, while I get your leash. We're going on a long walk because I have some things to talk you about," Henry told Lucky, for whom only the word "walk" seemed to be the operative thought. Lucky zoomed to the front door and waited expectantly.

Henry poured himself a glass of milk and downed a couple of the cookies his mother had baked in honor of Uncle Roger's return this evening. Then he grabbed the leash and was nearly out of the kitchen when the phone rang. He looked at the caller ID – Emily!

But the voice on the other end was clearly not Emily's. Henry wasn't sure who it was, although he could have sworn that he heard the words, "Hi, Henry."

"I'm sorry," Henry replied, "but I'm not sure who this is."

"Henry," the voice was now barely a croak, "it's me, Emily. I have strep throat. By the time I knew I couldn't go to school today it was too late to call your house. I'm so sorry I missed our meeting."

Henry was elated. Strep throat – *excellent!* Emily wasn't sick of me at all, she was just sick. He was instantly ashamed of his completely self-centered reaction, but still, it sure felt good to know that Emily had not stood him up because she no longer cared about him.

"That's okay," he said, "though I *was* kind of worried when you didn't show up. Are you feeling better?"

Emily tried to clear her throat, with little success. "Not really," she rasped. "The doctor says it will take a few days to clear up. But what I hate is that my dad and I can't go to the dinner tomorrow night. I was really looking forward to it."

Emily's words seared through Henry's brain like molten lava, shutting down every thought except for the fateful words – *can't go to the dinner tomorrow night, can't go to the dinner tomorrow night*. He was on the verge of saying, "Are you sure you can't make it?" when he caught himself. How thoughtless would that sound!

"No, no, of course you can't go," he agreed, but that was about all he could manage as he struggled to hide his disappointment.

"Henry," said Emily weakly, "I can't talk anymore; it hurts my throat too much. Call me on Sunday and tell me all about how much fun the dinner was."

Henry promised he would and slowly placed the phone back into its cradle. He could just imagine his report to Emily about how much "fun " the dinner was, starting with "Well, we got there and sat at a table all by ourselves."

He slumped at the kitchen counter for a few minutes, absorbing this new blow. But there was no way to continue indulging in such depressing thoughts in the face of Lucky's impatient barking, making clear that it was past time to go for their walk. Henry reluctantly rose, picked up the leash and snapped it onto the pup's collar. Together they headed out the door.

Lucky got quite an earful on their walk. "Well, Lucky, the Parent/Child dinner has just morphed back into the Parent/Child debacle," Henry explained as they strolled along their usual route. "I don't know a soul at school except for Emily and that is going to be abundantly clear when Uncle Roger and I get to the dinner and we don't have anyone to sit with."

Lucky rubbed up against Henry's leg, as he always did on their walks. But on this day that little affectionate nudge was just what Henry needed to feel that at least someone understood his problems. Even if that someone just happened to be a dog.

Henry and Lucky rambled along in silence. Despite having been informed about Henry's great dilemma, Lucky never varied from his usual high-spirited routine exploring everything in his path. Henry, on the other hand, was busily hatching a plan as they walked. He realized his only option was to convince his uncle that now that Emily had pulled out, they really didn't need to trouble themselves to go to the dinner at all. Wouldn't it be so much more fun to stay home with his mom and Lucky rather than being stuck with a bunch of random strangers? Of course it would! By the time they arrived home, Henry had completely convinced himself of the wisdom of his argument – there was clearly no point at all in going to the Parent/Child dinner.

CHAPTER 29

It took Henry and Lucky approximately a nanosecond after entering the house to realize that something was different. There was an electric current pulsing though the entire house that could only mean one thing – Uncle Roger was in residence. The sound of his thundering voice and his irrepressible laughter soon confirmed it.

Lucky tore into the kitchen and leapt into Uncle Roger's arms. Henry could not get over how completely the little dog had fallen for his uncle and Lucky received an equally warm welcome from Roger, who scratched him right behind the ears, which he somehow knew was Lucky's absolute favorite thing. Henry's greeting to his uncle was more measured – on one level he loved having his uncle back, but there was a big hurdle ahead. He needed to convince the convivial Uncle Roger that they really did not need to attend the Parent/Child dinner. Henry had his talking points all ready and, he was so sure they were compelling that he was actually thinking to himself *how hard could this possibly be*?

It turned out that it really wasn't hard at all, mainly because Uncle Roger never took a word that Henry said seriously. Oh sure, he understood they no longer had a pre-arranged table of people to sit with but as Uncle Roger countered, "That's the least of our concerns, Henry. We'll do just fine, don't you worry about a thing. Nothing is going to stop us from attending that dinner together and having a magnificent time, right?"

And with that Uncle Roger held out his enormous hand for a high five. Henry had no choice but to return the greeting, thus seeming to agree that they would indeed attend the dinner and have a "magnificent" time. So much, Henry thought dispiritedly, for his brilliant talking points.

As he trudged up the stairs to bed that night, Henry had little doubt that tomorrow he was in for one miserable evening. He entered his room and the first thing he saw was his too small jacket hanging there, the perfect reminder of what a mess was ahead. At least he could count on one small thing. He had reminded Uncle Roger that the dress for tomorrow evening was coat and tie. And Uncle Roger had assured him that was no problem – he had brought his best coat and tie just for this special occasion.

CHAPTER 30

As was his habit, Henry did not set an alarm on the weekend, but even without the insistent beeping he found himself wide awake much earlier than usual. He was simply too worried to sleep any longer. He glanced down and noticed that his concerns were not shared by Lucky, who was still snoring comfortably in his bed, clearly without a care in the world.

Henry propped himself up against his pillow, put his hands behind his head and tried to pinpoint what was really bothering him. As he parsed it through, he realized that what he was dreading the most was arriving at the dinner and being completely ignored, as if he didn't even exist at his new school. He hated picturing the look on his uncle's face when he finally had to admit that he really didn't have a friend in the world at school except Emily, who wasn't even there. And he could just feel the humiliation of watching all the other people at the dinner happily beckoning to each other to join their tables, while he and Uncle Roger had to spend the evening sitting alone.

His drab reverie was interrupted by Lucky, who had awakened and immediately jumped up onto Henry's bed in the hopes of a scratch behind the ears. Lucky was not disappointed as Henry, even in his gloomiest moments, was always happy to give Lucky his favorite rub.

At breakfast, Henry tried one more time to convince Uncle Roger they really didn't need to go the dinner, but his heart wasn't in it because he knew it was a losing battle. Which, of course, with Uncle Roger it was.

After he finished eating Henry went outside to work on the garden, with Lucky trailing happily along. Henry was not sure why, but somehow this garden had come to be very important to him. He had rounded off the corners of the plot to give it a better sense of style, added plans for a path to make harvesting easier and, despite the extra effort, decided to dig out another layer of clay to make room for even more topsoil. A lot of things had spun out of his control in his life over the past year, but this was one thing Henry could make his own, and since he was at last totally in charge of something, he was going to make it perfect. Except for a break for lunch he worked steadily until it was time to get ready for the dinner. The hard labor was the perfect antidote to keep his mind off what he knew was in store – a mortifying evening.

CHAPTER 31

Henry finished tying his tie exactly the way his dad had taught him, and tightened the knot firmly against his collar. His mom had surprised him with a new tie for the occasion and he had to admit that he liked the effect of the handsome splash of red against his crisp white shirt. He slipped on his blazer and surveyed himself in the mirror. Wearing a short-sleeved shirt definitely helped take the emphasis away from his too small jacket. If he hunched his shoulders just a little he could actually make the sleeves look longer, which he hoped he would remember to do. He certainly didn't want Uncle Roger to be embarrassed by his appearance. He smoothed his hair and adjusted his glasses.

"What do you think, Lucky? Do I look okay?" Lucky wagged his tail furiously, his version of a high five.

Henry found his mom in the kitchen, enjoying a late afternoon cup of tea. She echoed Lucky's approval saying, "Oh honey, you look wonderful!"

Since he had resigned himself to the inevitable, he saw no reason to ruin his mother's obvious pleasure that he and his uncle would be sharing this family outing, so he didn't bring up any of his worries about the evening. And besides, he had come up with a new plan. He and Uncle Roger would slip quietly into the room, find a table way in the back and simply fly under the radar until the dinner ended. With any luck at all, no one would even notice they were there. He poured himself a glass of milk and chatted with his mom about nothing in particular until they heard Uncle Roger coming down the stairs.

Roger swept into the kitchen with a broad smile; he was clearly looking forward to the evening. "Henry, I love that tie," he declared enthusiastically. "Red is your color! Now, are we all set to go?"

If Uncle Roger found the ensuing silence strange, he gave no indication of it. Henry, aghast, stared at him in disbelief, his only thought a stunned, "Oh no." Even his mom, whose tolerance for Roger's eccentricities seemed to have no limit, was rendered speechless.

Roger was indeed wearing a coat and tie, but neither one resembled the traditional meaning of those terms. His neckpiece was a bolo tie, the two black strings held together at his neck by an enormous silver and turquoise clasp. His jacket was buckskin, adorned front and back with fringe, along with

102

another helping of fringe on the cuffs. Here and there a random collection of beads and small colorful shells had been sewn into the material.

It was Uncle Roger who broke the silence. "How do you like my jacket?" he asked spinning around so that they could see every aspect of it, "it's my absolute favorite."

Mary recovered first. "Roger" she replied, "I have honestly never seen anything like it."

And Roger, who would never dream of judging anyone by what he or she was wearing, took this as a lovely compliment. "Thank you, Mary," he said with a pleased smile.

Only Lucky, who was as non-judgmental about a person's clothing as Uncle Roger, reacted normally, bounding toward Roger with unabated delight.

Henry really couldn't bring himself to say a word. His uncle looked like he was dressed more for a rodeo than a school dinner. Henry doubted Roger could have found a way to call more attention to himself had he worn a blinking red neon suit. But Uncle Roger, completely unperturbed and anxious to begin the evening, was hastening Henry out the door.

"C'mon, my boy," he said, "we don't want to miss a minute of this great adventure!" Henry shot his mother a stricken glance as he walked reluctantly out the door behind Roger. She shrugged sympathetically and blew him a kiss.

Henry watched the fringe on his uncle's coat sway in the evening breeze as they walked to the car, and he could hear the occasional clicks from the gentle collisions of the beads and shells. He would soon be at the school dinner with a buckskin-clad, 6 foot 3 force of nature. So much for flying under the radar, Henry thought, resigning himself at last to the worst.

CHAPTER 32

The school was awash in lights and the warm glow piercing the falling darkness gave the utilitarian cement building a festive air. Students and their parents or guests were streaming out of their cars in high spirits. Just as Henry had envisioned, as he and Uncle Roger approached the doors they could hear people calling to one another with invitations to sit together. Needless to say, none of those invitations was directed their way.

They found the check-in desk, picked up their nametags and walked into the bustling dining room. The friendly woman behind the desk had confirmed that there were no assigned tables, adding cheerfully, "You two just go right on in and sit with your friends." Her welcoming words felt like a rebuke to Henry who thought that it would be nice to comply with her directive, except for one little problem: I have no friends.

The room was full of tables, many already full but a few others completely vacant. Henry, who had observed plenty of surprised glances directed their way as people spied Uncle Roger in his unusual outfit, was relieved to see that there was an empty table right in the back of the room. He was about to grab this perfect bit of real estate in the equivalent of Siberia when he realized that Uncle Roger was no longer beside him. Instead, Roger was bearing down on a man and his son who had just walked in. They looked a bit unsure of themselves as they glanced uncertainly around in a way that made it obvious that they, too, had no pre-arranged place to sit. Henry cringed as he watched his uncle descend on the unsuspecting pair. It was clear from his usual expansive gestures that he was inviting them to sit with him and Henry. Henry fully expected them to issue a polite rejection and escape as quickly as they could get the words out of their mouths. But, no, they seemed quite content to follow Uncle Roger, who was by now cheerfully waving Henry over to an empty table he had chosen, right in the middle of the room.

"Henry," said Uncle Roger, "I want you to meet Labeeb Gupta and his son Ojayit. They are going to join us for dinner!"

Mr. Gupta, a small man in a dark suit – the complete opposite of Uncle Roger in virtually every way – asked in his lilting Indian accent, "Are you sure you have room for us and we are not imposing?" Imposing was a word that was not even in Uncle Roger's vocabulary and even Henry had to laugh to himself at the very notion that there was not room at their completely empty table. Roger assured them that he and Henry were delighted to have the pleasure of their company, and they all took their seats. But before anyone could say another word, Roger had jumped up, hastily excusing himself as he rushed off.

Henry and the Guptas watched as Roger made his way straight toward a woman and a girl who were standing in the back of the room. Even at this distance Henry could sense their discomfort. The woman was scanning the room hesitantly not sure where to go and the girl, very tall and ungainly, kept her eyes glued on the floor as if wishing herself to be anywhere but here. Henry recognized her instantly, how could he not? He had never met her but she was the tallest girl in school and everyone knew her by sight. He had no idea of her name. If the pair was taken aback by the sudden appearance of a tall, red-bearded stranger dressed in buckskin, Uncle Roger evidently was quickly able to assuage any of their concerns. He was pointing to his table and, as they nodded and started over, Henry saw a look of relief wash over the girl's face. He had the sudden revelation that he had not been the only one dreading the prospect of spending the evening sitting alone.

CHAPTER 33

Over the course of the next hour, as they each made trips to the various buffet stations, Uncle Roger effortlessly steered the conversation so skillfully that before long, no one felt like a stranger. Although their two newest dinner partners, Clara Gray and her daughter Chantelle had seemed painfully shy at first, overwhelmed at sitting with a group of people they had never met, they soon blossomed under Roger's gentle questioning and his genuine interest in them. Chantelle, as it turned out, played the violin and she and Uncle Roger were soon engaged in a spirited conversation about American fiddling. In addition to her classical violin, Chantelle also owned a fiddle with a slightly flattened bridge, the better to play the folk music that was clearly a favorite of hers. Henry was mesmerized as she spoke, her long fingers gesturing gracefully as she demonstrated the various techniques. Suddenly she didn't seem a bit awkward or gawky and he could just picture those strong, skillful fingers flying along the neck of her violin.

Uncle Roger next turned the conversation to, of all things, fencing. At first Henry felt embarrassed as he listened to his uncle's admiring description of his prowess with the épée, but the others seemed so interested and asked such good questions that he soon forgot his self-consciousness. No one would even think of calling me "Zorro" at this table! he found himself thinking. Mr. Gupta had actually practiced an Indian form of combat training in his youth, using wooden sticks to simulate swords in sparring matches. He and Henry had a fine time comparing notes, for just as in fencing, points in gatka are scored for touches on an opponent.

And then there was Ojayit. Small like his dad but stockier, he radiated an impish good nature. He tended to be quiet, not out of shyness but simply borne of his scientific preference for listening and observing rather than talking.

"Ojayit," asked Uncle Roger, drawing him casually into the conversation, "what's the first thing you usually do when you get home from school?"

Ojayit took the question very seriously. "Always first, I practice my judo." He grinned as he saw their surprise at his unlikely hobby and explained, "When you are small like I am….," leaving the obvious unsaid.

Then he shot his dad an affectionate glance of warning as he added, "And by the way, my friends call me 'Jay.'"

Mr. Gupta shook his head resignedly. "In our country names have a meaning," he said, "and in my own family in India we do not use nicknames. But here in the U.S...." He shrugged.

This was a topic right up Uncle Roger's alley. He held an unwavering belief that there was a deeper meaning in everyone and everything if only you took the time to find it, and he never failed to take the time. "What does Ojayit mean?" he asked with keen interest.

Mr. Gupta explained, "My wife and I thought a long time about a name for our son. We wanted him to have something he could carry proudly through life and so we chose Ojayit, which means 'courageous.'"

"And your name," Uncle Roger pressed on, fascinated, "what does Labeeb mean?" Mr. Gupta, so perfectly self-contained, laughed. "My mother must have had a crystal ball when she named me. Labeeb means 'sensible.'"

"Well," said Uncle Roger with a smile, "Names can be a two-edged sword. When I was visiting the Navajos a few years ago I met a man named Ata'Halne. I asked him about the meaning of his name and he said it meant, 'he interrupts.'"

Everyone was still laughing as Henry slipped away for a second helping of the exceptionally good roast beef.

As he returned with his heaping plate Henry heard Uncle Roger telling Jay and Chantelle that all of Henry's friends call him 'Uncle Roger' and they should, too.

"Isn't that right, Henry?" he asked as Henry put his heaping plate on the table. Henry confirmed that all of his friends absolutely did call him 'Uncle Roger,' not seeing any reason to add, all two of them.

CHAPTER 34

Henry was thoroughly enjoying the company and actually feeling remarkably relaxed when he spied Colby, who was headed toward the buffet but deliberately taking a route that would lead him right past Henry's table. As Colby strolled by their table Henry heard him signing in a low voice, "Da-vy, Da-vy Crockett, King of the Wild Fronti.."

Colby did not get the last syllable out. As quick as a cat, Uncle Roger sprang from his chair and blocked Colby's way. Colby suddenly looked very small next to towering Uncle Roger and Henry noted with immense satisfaction that Colby's habitual smirk had been replaced by a look of alarm. Colby realized he had been caught in the act and he glanced furtively toward his own table, hoping no one, especially his dad, was noticing. As usual, Uncle Roger did the unpredictable.

He put out his enormous right hand and said with a smile, "Hi, I'm Roger Caldwell, Henry's uncle." Henry suddenly had a horrible thought: please, please don't tell him to call you Uncle Roger. But Roger clearly had no such pleasantries in

112

mind as he listened to Colby sheepishly introducing himself in return.

"Have you and my nephew met?" Roger inquired politely. "Yyyessir," was all Colby could manage, gratefully withdrawing his aching hand from Roger's mighty grip.

Roger, still smiling and looking very imposing in his buckskin jacket, said affably, " I've always loved that Davy Crockett song. Whatever made you think to sing it?"

Colby, looking completely at sea, obviously could not give an honest answer like *gee, I was making fun of your crazy buckskin jacket,* so he ended up stammering, "Well, I was…it's just that…we, um, that is, my dad," - and here he had a sudden inspiration – "right, see, my dad was talking about Davy Crockett at our table and I just got the tune stuck in my head."

Not too bad for a lie made up on the fly, thought Henry, who was very much enjoying Colby's discomfiture.

"You have a nice singing voice, Colby," Uncle Roger continued. "Are you in the glee club?" Henry nearly laughed out loud, recalling Colby's disdain for the glee club.

"No sir," said Colby regaining his footing somewhat as he added, "I'm the captain of the football team."

"Ah," said Roger, "so, you're a leader of men. That's quite a responsibility." Colby just nodded and Roger continued, "I hear you have a big game coming up in a couple of weeks."

Henry was astounded. How on earth did his uncle know that? The game with West Plains, the Friday night after next, was the biggest of the year, an annual dogfight between the two long-time rivals. Again Colby could think of nothing better than a nod.

"Well, may the team with the best men win, Colby," Roger said, giving the quarterback a friendly clap on the shoulder. "And by the way," he added, "tell your dad to stop by our table if he has time – we can swap some memories about Davy Crockett."

Colby blanched, "Well, yeah, I'm sure he'd like to…if he has time, that is." Then, seeing his chance he added a hasty, "Nice to meet you," and made his scurried escape.

Henry barely noticed Colby's retreat. He was still trying to think through his uncle's unusual phrasing – not 'may the best team win,' but 'may the team with the best men win.' He wanted to ask about it, but by then Uncle Roger had settled into his seat and turned his full attention back to Mrs. Gray. "Now, Clara," he asked with his winning smile, "where were we?"

Henry noticed with great satisfaction that Colby took a very different route for his future trips to the buffet, giving Henry's table the widest possible berth, and Henry would bet good money that Colby's dad would NOT be stopping by their table to swap any memories about Davy Crockett. But, as much as Henry had enjoyed watching Colby's embarrassment, he had also felt a sense of dread. He knew Colby would find a way to exact his revenge as he always did, and Henry had no doubt that it would fall squarely on him. He still recalled Colby's parting words from their last encounter, "Just a preview of coming attractions."

CHAPTER 35

As the evening began to wind down Mrs. Gray, who had been the most reticent of the group, unexpectedly spoke up.

"Roger," she said in her soft, diffident voice, "I have been admiring your jacket all evening. I'm a seamstress by profession and quite honestly, I have never seen anything like the workmanship in your coat." Roger beamed at this heartfelt compliment and, knowing that he was talking to a true expert, told her what he had not previously shared about his buckskin jacket. The others at the table leaned forward listening intently, for Roger was an accomplished storyteller.

"This was a gift to me from a chief of a native American tribe in Arizona," he explained in an unusually quiet voice for him. "It's made of elk hide and all the stitches are so carefully sewn that none breaks the outer part of the skin, so it is completely waterproof, just as it was on that majestic animal. All the beads and shells have meaning and look here," he said as he directed Clara's hand to a spot just under the fringe on the left side over his heart. She felt a raised area under the buckskin – something had been sewn into the hide itself.

116

Clara looked at him questioningly. "That's an amulet. I have no idea what it is, nor must I ever try to uncover it or it will lose its power," said Roger. "It was put there as a gift to bring good fortune." Roger paused and looked around at his new friends adding, "And it worked because I met all of you tonight!"

Everyone laughed at this compliment that so neatly ended his story, but Henry found himself wondering whether that amulet in anyone else's hands would have had anywhere near the same effect as Uncle Roger's genuine sensitivity and kindness had accomplished this evening for a group of people who needed it most. A group, Henry had the insight to realize, that included him.

Unable to restrain himself with so much delicious food available after so many lean dinners at home, Henry made one last trip to the dessert bar. As he waited in line he looked over at his table, watching everyone talking and laughing together as if they had known each other for years instead of hours. He had always thought of his uncle as simply a nonstop talker, but tonight he saw that Uncle Roger was actually a thoughtful and accomplished conversationalist, able to bring out something interesting in everyone. The bigger mystery was how had Roger managed to assemble precisely the perfect mix of strangers together in the course of a single evening? That was something Henry decided needed some serious thought. It was evident how different their table looked compared to most of the others – the Guptas from India, Chantelle, the tallest girl in the school sitting next to the diminutive Jay, and of course, huge Uncle Roger himself unabashedly resplendent in his buckskin coat and bolo tie. Henry put an extra dollop of whipped cream on his hot fudge sundae and walked back to his table thinking something to himself he never would have imagined just a few hours earlier: *there is no place else I would rather be*.

As they made their goodbyes there was no mistaking that everyone had had a wonderful time. Mr. Gupta was handing Uncle Roger his business card and insisting he call next time he was in town. Uncle Roger was promising Mrs. Gray that when he next returned he would let her study his buckskin jacket to learn the secrets of the remarkable handiwork that had produced it. But what Henry really loved was hearing Jay say with complete confidence that his new pals would surely agree with him, "Hey Chantelle, Henry and I want to hear you play that violin! Let's get together soon."

The look on Chantelle's face as she agreed mirrored exactly the same unexpected thing that Henry was thinking: *I'm included!*

The ride home was too short for Henry and his uncle to have much of a conversation, although there were so many things Henry wanted to ask Uncle Roger about. Of course it was hard to get a word in since Roger was absorbed in offering a monologue about how wonderful the dinner had been and how great the food tasted and what very nice friends Henry had.

The only reason I have these very nice friends is thanks to you, Henry thought to himself, but in the short time left he was determined to turn the conversation to something that he had not really talked to anyone about before.

"You know, there are also some not so nice people at school," he said. "There's this one kid who gets bullied all the time by some of the bigger guys." This was the best he could do. He could not bring himself to admit that he was that kid who was bullied.

Uncle Roger was quiet for a few seconds, a world record for him. And then, as they were turning into the driveway he said, "Henry, I've always believed something a very wise philosopher once said because I know it to be true." He put the car in park and laid his hand on Henry's shoulder and said, "Only the weak are cruel."

CHAPTER 36

The next morning at breakfast Henry couldn't hide his disappointment. Uncle Roger had been called away suddenly and had departed so early in the morning that his only chance to say goodbye was a note addressed to Mary and Henry with a phone number scrawled across the bottom.

It read: *So sorry to rush off but something has come up. What a marvelous time we had – I will never forget it! Will try to return soon, but if you ever need me right away, call this number. Love, Roger.*

"Mom," Henry asked, "what does Uncle Roger actually do? His mother, who was folding the note and putting it into a kitchen drawer for safekeeping, simply shook her head. "Honey, I have no idea."

They enjoyed their traditional weekend pancakes and Henry told his mom all about the evening, including how Uncle Roger seemed to have a sixth sense that enabled him to identify exactly the people who should join them for dinner. Henry felt sheepish when he admitted how embarrassed he had been about

Uncle Roger's attire, especially because it was so clear to him now that Roger's inclusiveness and kindness transcended whatever he was wearing, something that the Guptas and the Grays had instantly understood. His mom agreed. "I think we both learned something yesterday," she said with a wry smile.

After breakfast Henry called Emily. He knew she would be wondering how the dinner went and he had been worrying about whether she was feeling better. He was delighted to hear her answer the phone in an almost normal voice. He gave her the short version of the dinner, promising to fill in all the important details when they met in person. She would be back in school tomorrow she promised, and they both looked forward to resuming their usual meeting between the fourth and fifth periods.

Later that afternoon Mary joined Henry and Lucky in the garden. She was impressed with the progress Henry had made in clearing the plot. And she was equally struck by how much bigger and stronger Henry had become as he wielded his pick and lifted the heavy clay, even though he himself didn't seem to realize it. She made a mental note: buy Henry new clothes!

That night, as he lay in bed after soothing his sore muscles in a long, hot shower, Henry played back the entire school dinner in his head. He was still pretty shocked at how well the evening had turned out. Left to his own devices he would have hunkered down alone at a table in the back of the room, hoping no one noticed him or his flamboyant uncle. But Uncle Roger, left to his own devices, picked a table in the middle of the room, assembled a congenial group of what turned out to be his new friends, and frankly didn't care what anyone in the room thought about him or what he was wearing. He simply cared about the people he was with, and he made it a memorable evening for every one of them, Henry included.

But, there was something else:

Henry could not get over the fact that Uncle Roger, as kind and thoughtful as he always was, didn't let Colby get away with his mean-spirited Davy Crockett prank for even one second. Roger had confronted Colby instantly and made him face up to what he was doing, seeing right through Colby's lies. Of course, thought Henry, maybe it's not so hard to do that when you tower over your tormentor. Henry figured that if he were a foot taller and as strong as his uncle, Colby, the consummate bully, would never have bothered him in the first place. But – and Henry was being brutally honest with himself here – since he was a glasses-wearing, thin, new kid whose best athletic skill was fencing, he was the perfect fodder for this well-practiced taunter.

He was nearly asleep when suddenly he sat straight up, inspired again by the memory of Uncle Roger's immediate response to Colby's taunt. In that instant a new resolve about Colby's bullying came over him, as clear as a clarion: This is going to stop!

CHAPTER 37

Henry walked to school on Monday morning with mixed feelings. He was very anxious to see Emily and also hoping to run into Jay and Chantelle. Just the thought of seeing kids who would be equally glad to see him gave him a warm feeling that he hadn't really felt since he and his mom had moved here. But there was also a sense of – he hated to admit it – fear. It scared him when Colby and his teammates accosted him and the fact that he could never think of a good response made him feel even worse. He tried to recall his resolve of the night before, but exactly how he was going to stop Colby's bullying was something that, in the cold light of day, eluded him.

Henry had not been in the building for even five minutes before he ran into Jay. It felt so good, although completely unusual, to hear someone other than Emily say, "Hey Henry, I've been looking for you!"

Jay had indeed been searching for Henry. With his typical attention to detail, he had checked the master schedule online and found that he and Henry shared the same lunch period.

"Henry," said Jay in his quiet yet confident way, "let's have lunch together. We have lots to talk about."

And Henry, who had spent every lunch period since school had started sitting alone said, "Sure, Jay, that would be great" as if he got such invitations all the time. But he felt dazed as he realized that today, for the first time, he would walk into the lunchroom and a friend would be waiting.

Before they parted, Jay told Henry that he had also looked up Chantelle's schedule, only to find that her lunch period differed from theirs. But, as Jay assured Henry, he would catch up with Chantelle at some point today and let her know that he and Henry hadn't forgotten that she owed them a violin concert. Henry nodded his agreement; he would love to hear Chantelle play the violin and he could just imagine her pleasure at finding that "he" and Jay had remembered, although of course it was Jay who was making sure to touch base with Chantelle. He was impressed that Jay was willing to foster their friendships so openly and unguardedly without seeming to worry a bit about being rejected. Just like, Henry suddenly realized, Uncle Roger had done at the dinner.

Henry and Emily made the most of their short meeting time, with Henry doing most of the talking as he fleshed out all the best details of the dinner. Emily got a laugh out of Uncle Roger's confrontation with Colby and made Henry promise to be sure and count her in for Chantelle's violin concert. She didn't know who Jay was, but like nearly everyone in the school, she was well aware of Chantelle, though they had never met. Emily looked a bit pale and admitted to still feeling kind of tired, but she was glad to be back at school and their visit, brief as it was, was a tonic to them both.

When Henry arrived at his locker at the end of the day, he was feeling better than he had since he started at this new school. Lunch with Jay had been fun and actually pretty interesting, too, as Jay had brought some extra helpings of his mother's homemade samosas just to share with Henry. Henry had never tasted these Indian specialties, and he became an instant fan of the fried pastries with their savory filling of peas, potatoes, and onions made fragrant with ginger, garlic and coriander.

But now, as he packed up his books, he found himself feeling increasingly apprehensive. It was Monday, the team's day off from practice and Henry fully expected to see Colby and company appear any second, especially after the events of the dinner. He started packing his things more quickly in the hopes of making a quick getaway, but then stopped himself. This was no way to live. Henry forced himself to slow down and he actually hung around a bit longer than was necessary,

126

ready to confront this issue head on. But there was no issue to confront as Colby and his gang never showed up.

As he walked home, Henry could not help but wonder whether Colby had been so intimidated by Uncle Roger that he just decided to give up on Henry. He half hoped it was true, and half hoped that it wasn't, because he hated the thought that it was his uncle, not he, who had put a halt to the bullying.

CHAPTER 38

But Henry had the good sense not to fret over the end of being bullied, no matter what might have stopped it. Over the course of the rest of the week he put all concerns about Colby out of his mind and simply enjoyed his visits with Emily, his lunches with Jay (who was now hooked on Henry's mom's chocolate chip cookies) and their occasional meetings with Chantelle between classes. Chantelle really could not be missed as she traveled the halls towering over everyone, both boys and girls, and many of the teachers, for that matter. She confessed to Henry and Jay that she hated being so tall. But she had long past given up slouching to seem shorter – and she was honest enough to admit that having Jay and Henry as friends who didn't care about her height gave her confidence to face the constant snickers from the other kids at school, which made them both feel even more protective than ever of her feelings. Jay, as usual, made them laugh as he offered to take at least 5 inches from Chantelle and add it to his own short stature. For reasons that he didn't completely understand, Henry was unable to share his own story about Colby's bullying with his new friends. He felt embarrassed by it and he wondered if they would think less of him because he was such an easy target.

Over the weekend, as the sun lowered earlier each day and the temperatures dropped ever more steadily after dusk, Henry hastened to finish the garden. It was time to start getting these plants into the ground so they would mature before the first killing frost and he was determined that his mom was going to have the most bountiful winter garden ever, even as he hated the thought of eating some of it. He filled the large area that he had so painstakingly dug out with black, loamy topsoil and then hauled up some old bricks he found in the shed to lay out the path. He had spent time on the Internet looking at gardens and had found a herringbone pattern for the brick path that he thought would give it a particularly distinctive look.

By late Sunday afternoon the garden was ready and Henry and Mary spent the next couple of hours planting lettuce, spinach, radishes, broccoli, cauliflower, beets, kale, potatoes, and, for a gourmet touch, arugula. Uncle Roger had provided them with plants, nestled in deep trays filled with rich, dark soil to be sure and give the plants a head start on the cold growing season. As usual, somehow Roger knew that because winter gardens must mature before the first frost, time was of the essence. Henry and his mom finished their work just as darkness was falling, and they stood for a quiet few minutes surveying the garden as it slowly disappeared in the waning light, each picturing how abundant it would surely look in just a couple of months. Henry felt an odd pang of regret that his days of hard labor were over. Lately even he had started to notice that his shirts were fitting more tightly across his shoulders and biceps, and his muscles no longer ached after a day spent wielding the pickaxe.

CHAPTER 39

Monday dawned cold and rainy. Lucky made his displeasure with the weather clear by insisting on seriously abbreviating their walk but Henry welcomed the soggy weather, happy that the garden was getting a good soaking. He hunched forward against the raw northwest wind as he made his way to school, filled with the satisfaction of finishing up the garden project and the pleasant anticipation (he still hadn't gotten used to this) of seeing his friends at school.

The day passed quickly. At lunch Jay was full of plans for Chantelle's "concert debut," as he had now taken to calling it. He had spoken with his parents and they agreed that it would be wonderful to have everyone come to their house to listen to Chantelle play her violin and then enjoy a luncheon featuring his mom's favorite Indian dishes. Henry was particularly interested in Jay's description of palak chaat, Mrs. Gupta's fried spinach, thinking he might finally have found the perfect way to use all that spinach they were unfortunately about to grow.

By the time the final bell had sounded, the rain had stopped and the sun was shining. As he finished putting the last of his books into his backpack and cinched the straps, Henry was thinking of nothing more than how pleasant his walk home was going to be compared to the morning's wet slog. He was completely unprepared for the rough shove that sent him stumbling into the lockers. But he had no doubt whom he was going to see when he finally regained his balance and turned around. Colby.

"Hello, Caldwell," Colby said almost conversationally, "Gosh, we've missed you." He was standing surrounded by his usual group of players, wearing his shirt with the "C" and sporting his invariable smirk. "How's your hillbilly Uncle Buckskin doing?"

Just at that moment, Emily came walking around the corner.

Looking back, Henry was never sure whether it was the appearance of someone who believed that he was "very brave" or the sudden, visceral anger he felt at Colby's insulting reference to Uncle Roger, but his resolve to put an end to this misery surfaced with a vengeance.

"Still wearing your coward shirt, I see," he said to the surprised Colby as he adjusted his glasses and looked closer as if to see the shirt better. "Yep, the coward shirt actually fits you better than ever.

"You know," he continued, "if you had any guts, Colby, you wouldn't need half a football team behind you when you pick on someone. Why don't you and I settle this once and for all? Let's step outside and fight it out one on one, like… and here Henry paused for effect…real men." Henry waited just a second before adding, "Or are you too chicken to do anything but sneak up on people and hit them from behind?"

Colby looked shocked, not just because he didn't think Henry had it in him to stand up for himself, but also because he had absolutely no doubt that he could tear Henry apart.

"Caldwell, are you nuts? I could take you down with one hand tied behind my back," the big quarterback boasted. Some of the team members looked uncomfortable, but not one said a word.

Henry leaned back casually against his locker, looking as relaxed as though they were discussing the weather rather than planning to engage in a pitched battle. "That won't be necessary, Colby," he said with a dismissive smile. "You can use both hands, but it's just you and me, no help from your teammates."

Colby looked at his watch and shrugged. "Fine, Caldwell, it's your funeral. We meet in ten minutes on the old practice field. That'll give you time to say your prayers." And with that he stalked off, his followers dutifully bringing up the rear.

Emily was appalled.

"Henry, this is crazy," she said with alarm. "You can't just go to a field and fight him. He's huge and he's mean and he could...," she hesitated, not wanting to describe all the ways Henry could get mauled by the big quarterback. "Well, I don't know what he might do," she finished more diplomatically, "but this is *not* a good idea."

Actually, Henry couldn't have agreed more, but he wasn't going to admit this to Emily. He was still trying to figure out what made him challenge Colby to a fistfight, something, come to think of it, he had never actually done. But there was no going back now.

Emily had another thought, "If only you had an invisibility cloak," she offered as a last resort. The thought made Henry laugh despite the dire circumstances. "Emily," he said with a shrug, "not everyone can be a wizard."

Seeing Emily's apprehension he added, "I'll be fine," with more confidence than he actually felt. "You just wait right here. I don't want you out there."

"Well, that's not going to happen," Emily replied feistily with a shake of her head. "If Colby is going to have all his teammates out there cheering him on, you're going to have a cheering section, too."

134

The Love Rock Chronicle

CHAPTER 40

The old practice field had not seen any use since the school built a new field a few years back. Now it was just a weedy mess, but it was far enough off the beaten path that it was unlikely any of the teachers would discover what they were doing. It was an inspired choice by Colby – the old field was the perfect place to hold a fight in private.

Colby was totally into it as Henry and Emily approached, joking with the other players, posing with his fists up like the old-time boxers used to do, and clearly enjoying himself. Henry, on the other hand, was summoning all of his will power to appear calm and unconcerned, but he could not stop his heart from beating wildly and to his dismay, his breathing was shallow and fast. He hoped no one noticed.

Without a word they squared off, each circling warily trying to take the measure of the other. The players stood stolidly on one side and Henry's lone supporter Emily, clutching her jacket tightly against both the chilly air and her own fears for Henry, stood alone on the other.

Colby, as he had proven time and again, did not have a subtle bone in his body and this trait carried straight over into his fighting style. He began his attack immediately, flinging his fists in a wild flurry at Henry without any plan or discipline.

And just as quickly Henry realized that there were remarkable parallels between fighting and fencing. All the skills that he had learned over the years to avoid being touched by an opponent's blade were equally useful to avoid being hit by Colby's erratic swipes. And on the increasing occasions that Henry, who chose his moments carefully, landed his own well-placed blows, he could see they hit their mark, as Colby winced and pulled back. As they continued to spar, Henry's confidence grew in direct proportion to Colby's increasingly frenzied aggravation that this fight was not the easy walkover that he had imagined.

Finally, visibly tiring from expending so much ineffectual effort and allowing his frustration to get the better of him, Colby made a desperate lunge at Henry, determined to deliver a knockout punch. But a lunge, of all things, was a classic fencing move that Henry had repelled a thousand times before and this time was no exception. He nimbly stepped to the side and as Colby lost his balance, Henry, surprising even himself with his newfound strength, grabbed him and threw him to the ground, knocking the wind out of him.

As Henry jumped on top of his gasping opponent, he was overcome with rage – at the loss of his father, at having to move away from everything he loved, at all of Colby's hurtful taunts inflicted for no good reason – and suddenly he wanted nothing more than to pummel Colby with all his might. In that blind moment of fury Henry reached down and grabbed a rock, the better to inflict serious pain. Colby, his energy spent, knew he was defenseless and he curled himself into a ball, hoping to shield as much of his body as possible against this sure onslaught.

Henry brought his hand high above his head, glancing back at it just as he prepared to deliver the devastating blow. But that brief look, perhaps only a second or two at most, brought everything to a halt.

Henry saw that he was holding a rock shaped perfectly like a heart. And instantly that sight stayed his hand and he felt his rage seep away. He shook his head as if to clear away a bad dream and, revolted by what he had been about to do, he leapt to his feet, slipping the rock into his pocket.

All was silent. Colby was still curled in a defensive position, hands covering his head, expecting the worst. Henry straightened his glasses. "I've had enough, Colby," he said quietly. "Let's call it a draw."

Colby uncurled himself and looked up in surprise, unable for a few seconds to figure out what had happened. But then he realized that the fight was over. He rose slowly to his feet and faced Henry. Colby was only too aware that this fight had not ended in a draw and he felt humiliated in front of his teammates, a very new experience for him.

Henry extended his hand. "Let's call an end to this, Colby. No more taunts, no more mean tricks. Let's just leave each other alone. Agreed?"

Colby's hands hung by his side, his shirt and pants covered with mud and grass. He glanced at his teammates who stood watching silently. How, he wondered, could he save face? He harbored no illusions that Henry had won the fight, but now he had a real decision to make and for Colby it was all about what was best for him. His mind raced through the possibilities and then he made his fateful decision.

He could not show weakness. He raised his hands and then deliberately put them into his pockets, leaving no doubt that he was spurning Henry's offer of a truce.

But to Henry's surprise, he felt a hand grasp his. The big lineman, who had looked uncomfortable so many times when Colby was bullying Henry but had never said a word, stepped forward to shake Henry's hand.

"Agreed, Henry," he said quietly. Then he turned to the other players. "Let's go guys," he said, adding, "you too, Colby." They walked off, with Colby trailing behind.

CHAPTER 41

Henry watched them go, feeling almost in shock. Had he actually won the fight? Was he truly still in one piece? Had he really gotten an agreement from the team to stop the taunting? His mind was spinning.

The entire fight now seemed a blur to him and he reached into his pocket to feel his heart rock to assure himself it all had really happened. The solid rock was there in his pocket and he wrapped his hand tightly around it – yes, it had really happened.

He was so deep in thought that he didn't feel the first gentle touch on his arm. Emily stood by his side searching for words – she, too, was trying to make sense about what had happened. She was no fan of fighting, that was for sure, but she understood Henry's need to bring the miserable confrontations with Colby to an end and nothing would have stopped her from being right there to support him. She had felt scared when Henry picked up the rock and greatly relieved when he ended the fight without another blow. But, why, she wondered, why had he so suddenly stopped the fight?

Henry was still lost in a daze. She touched his arm again, more forcefully this time and said, "Henry?" He came to, as if from a dream, and looked at her distractedly. She searched his face, which seemed strangely blank, "Are you okay?" she asked worriedly.

Her question brought Henry back – *am I okay?* – but he needed a moment to collect his thoughts before he could answer. To gain time, Henry fell back on his old habit and reached up to straighten his glasses, though for once they were actually perfectly straight. He was glad Emily was there. It was a relief to be able to explain what had happened to someone who already knew about love rocks.

"Emily," he said slowly in a hushed tone, "I was absolutely going to hit Colby with a rock, I was honestly that furious. But when I looked at it..," he paused almost not believing what he was about to say.

Emily, I saw it plain as day - it was shaped like a heart. It made me hate what I was about to do and that's why I stopped." He shook his head, as if he couldn't believe it himself, then added, "I have the rock right here in my pocket."

Emily understood instantly. A love rock! She could still see Uncle Roger on the day of their hike holding that heart-shaped rock that he had found and telling them, "It holds the power of love." She would never forget it. "Can I see it?" she asked.

142

Henry reached into his pocket and drew out the rock. He held it in his palm and they stared at it wordlessly.

After a few seconds Emily broke the silence, unable to hold back any longer. "Henry, for some reason...I...I just don't see the heart shape." Henry was still studying the rock, thinking the same thing. He moved it every which way, but nothing he did made it look even remotely like a heart. It looked exactly like what it was, a plain, ordinary rock, nothing special.

Henry was dumbfounded. "Emily, I swear I saw a heart!" He raised his hands in disbelief and asked, "Why else would I have stopped fighting?" Emily had no answer.

CHAPTER 42

As Henry walked home he became more and more agitated. What was it about these love rocks that seemed to elude him? Why could he not see the heart shape when everyone else did, then manage to see one when it wasn't even there? He played that moment in the fight over and over in his mind – grabbing the rock, raising it high, glancing up and seeing...seeing what? Did he really see a heart? He was sure he had and it was a perfect heart shape, but when he tugged the rock out of his pocket, it remained just what it was when he and Emily had viewed it, a shapeless piece of stone. He tried to convince himself that it made no difference – heck, he won the fight, didn't he? But like a pebble in a shoe, this small thing was causing him pain.

His spirits were lifted, as always, by the unfailingly excited welcome from Lucky. A lot has changed for both of us since we found each other, he thought to himself as he snapped on Lucky's leash. During their leisurely stroll, Henry gave Lucky a rundown on the events of the day, as much to clarify them in his own mind as to inform Lucky. And, against all logic, he even tried slipping the rock out of his pocket and looking at it as quickly as he could to simulate his fleeting glance at it during the fight. Maybe that was how he had managed to see the heart shape. But despite trying this twice, the rock did not reveal even the slightest inclination to look like a heart.

Back home, sitting at the kitchen table with a glass of milk and a couple of chocolate chip cookies close at hand, Henry laid the rock on the table. He studied it from every angle. Nothing. Again he was tempted to just forget about it – after all, he had bested Colby and gotten an agreement with the team leave him alone – why even bother worrying about the shape of a stone. And yet… he couldn't shake the feeling that he was missing something important.

Henry walked to the counter to get one more cookie and noticed the drawer where his mom had put Roger's farewell note. Suddenly his uncle's words came back to him with a jolt, *"but if you ever need me right away, call this number. Love, Roger."* And a single thought reverberated over and over in Henry's mind: I need you right away.

Henry held the note in his hand and looked at the phone number. Should he really call his uncle about this? Was it even important? He had no idea where Roger was and for all Henry knew, his uncle might be in the middle of something very critical. Then again, Uncle Roger had written the words, *but if*

you ever need me right away, call this number, and he never
said things he didn't mean. Henry picked up the phone and
dialed the number.

It rang only once before he heard his uncle's unmistakable
thunderous voice and usual greeting, "Henry, my boy, I love
you!" As much as Henry felt relieved to hear his uncle's voice,
he still could not bring himself to respond in kind.

"Hi Uncle Roger," was Henry's wan offering in return.
There might have been an awkward silence with anyone other
than his uncle, but Roger had never known the meaning of
awkward silences. He didn't let a second go by before he told
Henry that he was "in the very far West," but absolutely adored
hearing from him.

"Henry, what can I do for you?" he concluded in such a
casual way that made it seem as if nothing was more important
to him than this conversation. It put Henry instantly at ease.

Inspired by his uncle's welcoming tone, Henry spilled out
everything he had not been able to say to anyone – about the
bullying from Colby, his embarrassment at seeming to be such
an easy target, how Uncle Roger's confrontation with Colby
had made him determined to stand up to his nemesis, and
finally, how he had challenged Colby to a fight and saw – or
maybe didn't see – a love rock.

Uncle Roger was uncharacteristically quiet at the end of Henry's recitation. So quiet that Henry wondered if the line had gone dead somewhere in the middle of his one-sided conversation.

But then his uncle cleared his throat, and in an unusually quiet voice said, "Henry, let me tell you something that I know to be true. Just like love itself, love rocks can't be put into a predictable box as if they are all are exactly alike. Nothing in this life stays the same, much as we might wish it. Not even the most important loves of our lives, as we learned when…" his uncle's voice caught and there was silence for a few moments before he was able to continue "…when we lost your dad. But there is one thing that never changes, and that is power of love. That power is what has motivated all good people through the centuries. It is what moves us to do right to this day. Never underestimate it"

Uncle Roger paused again, and then asked, "Do you still have the love rock from the fight?" Henry said yes, it was right there in front of him, shapeless as ever. Uncle Roger asked him to hold it in one hand and write down what he was about to say. Henry held the rock, grabbed a pencil, and wrote the single sentence that Uncle Roger dictated. And then they said goodbye.

Henry read the words over and over, not sure what they meant.

CHAPTER 43

The music drifted over the audience as soft as the touch of a silken scarf. Henry watched in awe as Chantelle's fingers moved confidently over the strings of her violin, the bow a mesmerizing blur. Somehow this combination produced the most impossibly lovely sounds. Henry had never in his life experienced a private concert, and he was stunned at the power of live music. He wasn't alone. Chantelle's audience sat in rapt silence, moved by the beauty and intensity of her performance. The standing ovation at the end lasted so long that Chantelle, blushing with pride and embarrassment, had to implore them to stop. They urged her to play an encore and for that she grabbed her folk music fiddle. "This one is for Uncle Roger," she said with a grin as she launched into a spirited rendition of Take Me Home Country Roads. Henry had to laugh – how Uncle Roger would have loved this!

Henry was filling his plate one last time with the food on Mrs. Gupta's – was there any other way to describe it – phenomenal buffet table. He was thinking that if Jay ate these wonderful things every day he was the luckiest guy on earth.

Jay soon disabused him of that notion, saying his mother had been cooking these special dishes, a few of which he had never even tasted himself, for the past week, loving this rare chance to share all of her favorite foods from her native India with their new friends. Henry, who could hardly believe he was going back for seconds of spinach, of all things (though who wouldn't if spinach could always be fried to this level of perfection), along with another helping of the delectable butter chicken, settled himself in a corner chair overlooking the comfortable family room where everyone had gathered.

As he ate he watched with amusement as Eddie trailed behind Chantelle, completely enthralled by her and, as usual, full of questions. Eddie was proclaiming, "When I grow up I want to be as tall as you and play the violin." Henry smiled as Chantelle reached down to give Eddie a hug saying, "Well, Eddie, at least one of those wishes is within your own power to achieve."

In a far corner of the room Emily and Jay were engaged in a deep conversation and people were starting to crowd around Chantelle with praise for her performance, her height clearly the last thing in the world that mattered to them. In the kitchen, Henry's mom and Mrs. Gupta were having a spirited discussion about cooking. They were obviously planning to share recipes as Henry caught snatches of their questions to each other about

Indian spices and which were the best chocolate chips. But it was the expression on his mom's face that stopped him cold – she looked relaxed and happy. Henry had rarely seen that look since his dad died and he suddenly realized his mom had been every bit as lonely and sad as he had been, if not more. He felt guilty just thinking about how much he had relied on her resilience to get him through those devastating months without even considering how hard it must have been for her just to press on each day. How could he have been so oblivious? Was he really that out of it?

Just then, Emily came strolling over.

"Henry, what are you doing over here all by yourself?" she asked as she sat down beside him.

"Just trying to eat as much of Mrs. Gupta's awesome food as I can," Henry answered lightly. He wasn't in the mood to get into any deep discussions. And, he hadn't yet told Emily about his talk with Uncle Roger and his uncle's cryptic message. He was still trying to figure it out himself.

Emily observed the festivities for a few moments. "I wish he were here today," she said quietly.

Henry knew exactly what she meant. This party only happened because Uncle Roger had brought them all together. As they listened to the animated conversations and the laughter and watched people enjoying each other's company, Henry turned to Emily. "He is," he replied.

CHAPTER 44

Before turning in for the night Henry spent a few minutes examining what he had now come to think of as his "so-called" love rock, giving it one last chance to declare itself as heart-shaped. As usual, it stubbornly declined. Henry shrugged, climbed into bed, switched on the bedside lamp, and unfolded the piece of paper on which he had written Uncle Roger's message.

He read it over again: *This is the rock that unlocked the love hidden in a heart of stone.*

When he had first heard those words, just a few days ago in the kitchen, Henry had assumed that the "heart of stone" was the love rock itself. Pretty simple, though the rock was sure not much of a heart. But, as he thought more about it, he wasn't so sure. Lately he had started to wonder, could the heart of stone actually be his own heart?

Henry had never thought of himself as cold-hearted but there was no doubt that over these last few months, grief and loneliness had taken its toll. He was still smarting from realizing how little support he had given to his mom in the dark days and months after losing his dad. His face heated with shame as recalled her saying 'your uncle calls every few days to check on us' at the exact same time he was arguing that Uncle Roger should absolutely not go to the Parent-Child dinner. He hadn't even been aware of those calls that were such a comfort to his mother and he hated to think of how many good things would not have happened had he won that selfish argument.

Since he was being completely honest with himself, he also had to admit that he wasn't a bit proud of his decision to be cold and aloof at school, a dumb stunt that had nearly cost him his friendship with Emily. He honestly believed that he wasn't really like that, yet he had done it nonetheless – how could he square those two opposites of himself? And Henry was still stunned at the depth of his rage at Colby on the day of their fight. Good lord, was he really just seconds away from beating a defenseless boy with a rock?

By now he had built a strong case that it was his own heart that Uncle Roger meant when he referred to a heart of stone and there was no going back. Henry rose and walked to his dresser. He picked up his love rock, got back into bed and turned out the light. As he held it he repeated his uncle's message. *This is the rock that unlocked the love hidden in a heart of stone.* And in that instant Henry understood.

Uncle Roger, in his unorthodox way, had given him the puzzle and the solution in one deft sentence. Roger's words had, as his uncle knew they would, impelled Henry to decipher the meaning of "heart of stone" and it had ultimately led straight to his own heart.

But, of course, with Uncle Roger, it could not possibly end there. Henry recalled what his uncle had said to him the day they returned from the hike, when Henry was so disappointed about the fact that he couldn't see a love rock: Don't worry Henry, you'll see it when you need to.

Now he had finally figured it out. He saw exactly what Uncle Roger meant.

When he raised his hand in that blind rage against Colby, Henry realized that what he had actually seen, embodied in a heart of stone, was a choice. And when he stopped the fight it was because, in that single fateful second in time, he had made the right choice: to let the power of love win out.

He no longer cared that the rock that he held in his hand was not perfectly shaped like a heart. It was without a doubt a love rock. It had led him to unlock the love hidden in his own heart of stone.

And there was something else, something that made Henry feel a warm sense of pride. It was clear that Uncle Roger had never doubted that when the time came, Henry would make the right choice. That was why he made his confident prediction, "Don't worry Henry, you'll see it when you need to."

And so he had. Henry was still holding his love rock as drowsiness set in and sleep overcame him.

CHAPTER 45

Henry was astounded at how many weeds had invaded the garden, seemingly overnight. Leaning on his hoe, he surveyed the neat rows of burgeoning vegetables, now being choked by weeds from every direction. It was nearly 3:30 on a Sunday afternoon in early October and he knew he'd better get started if he had any hope of finishing the job before nightfall. Clouds were massing in the pewter sky and a light drizzle was already falling.

Henry worked steadily and methodically, taking satisfaction in seeing the rich, black soil re-emerge from beneath its blanket of unwanted green. The pile of weeds in his wheelbarrow grew. He quickened his pace as the pale gray light dimmed. It was getting harder and harder to see and he certainly wouldn't want to accidently dig up one of those precious beets! But even with his best efforts, it was completely dark by the time he emptied the last load of weeds into the ravine.

He was tired and wet – the drizzle had never let up – and he shivered as the chilly air seeped through his damp clothing.

Still, he didn't want to go inside quite yet. He had not lived in a cold climate until he and his mom had moved to this town, so he had never experienced fall weather that brought increasingly chilly days and nights that turned colder with each passing week. The promise of snow in the coming months excited him. It was something he was looking forward to. He clasped his arms across his chest to ward off the cold as he realized that looking forward was something he thought he had lost forever. But now looking forward was…

His thoughts were interrupted by his mom, who was calling through the open door, "Henry, your Uncle Roger is on the phone, can you come speak to him?"

Henry kicked off his muddy shoes outside the door and hurried inside. The warmth of the kitchen enveloped him as he took the phone, careful to hold it slightly away from his ear to mitigate as best he could the effect of Uncle Roger's impossibly loud voice. "Hi Uncle Roger," he said.

As usual, his uncle's familiar greeting came booming through the receiver, "Hello, Henry, my boy, I love you."

And, without even pausing to think Henry replied, "I love you, too."

THE END

Made in the USA
Middletown, DE
12 August 2020

15056165R00099